James Summers

The Rudiments of the Chinese Language

with dialogues, exercises, and a vocabulary

James Summers

The Rudiments of the Chinese Language
with dialogues, exercises, and a vocabulary

ISBN/EAN: 9783337392628

Printed in Europe, USA, Canada, Australia, Japan

Cover: Foto ©Andreas Hilbeck / pixelio.de

More available books at **www.hansebooks.com**

THE

RUDIMENTS

OF THE

CHINESE LANGUAGE,

WITH

DIALOGUES, EXERCISES, AND A VOCABULARY.

BY THE

REV. JAMES SUMMERS,

PROFESSOR OF CHINESE IN KING'S COLLEGE, LONDON.

LONDON:

BERNARD QUARITCH, 15 PICCADILLY.

1864.

PREFACE.

THE following little Manual is intended to supply a want, which it is believed that many feel, who leave this country to visit China for the first time. No small work having issued from the press that would at once acquaint a person with the nature of the Chinese language, and would also enable him to make a start in the acquisition of it, Mr. Quaritch determined on publishing this present little book to supply the deficiency, and in sequel to his other similar publications on Arabic, Persian, Turkish, and other languages. The Author hopes that Chinese scholars will excuse the defects which have occasionally crept in through the scarcity of Chinese type in this country, and the difficulty attending the compositor's work in such a language; and as this is an attempt to put Chinese into a European dress by the use of Roman type, the paucity of Chinese characters in the work will be of little consequence. Sufficient, however, has been given to enable the beginner to make himself master of the rudiments of the language, and, as he proceeds, he will find other works of a more complete character necessary, where he will meet with the signs which may be here dispensed with.

The Vocabulary at the end of the book consists of many most valuable words and phrases, which have been drawn from the work of the Rev. Joseph Edkins, entitled "*Progressive Lessons in Chinese,*" and which the Author here takes the opportunity to recommend to students of Chinese.

Hitchin, Herts,
　　Feb. 10, 1864.

INTRODUCTION.

1. THE Chinese language, with its numerous dialects, has no alphabet. It is written by means of characters, each of which represents an entire syllable. These syllables are simple, and are easily pronounced. They consist either of one vowel,—of a consonant and a vowel,—or of a consonant, a vowel, and a final consonant. There are no difficult combinations of consonants, as in the European tongues, nor accumulations of vowels as in some languages. The initial sounds, *ch, sh, ts,* and the final sound *ng,* may not be regarded as exceptions to this remark.

2. The Chinese characters are formed of very simple elementary figures or symbols. Their first rudiments are simple strokes or lines, and the point or dot. An infinite variety of forms is produced by the perpendicular, the horizontal, the oblique dash to the right, the oblique sweep to the left, and the large point like a comma. All the strokes required in writing are to be seen in the characters *yŭng,*[a] and *í*[b].

[a] 永 or 永 [b] 衣

3. When a number of simple forms, as *k'eù*,[a] 'mouth,' *jìn*,[b] 'man,' *jì*,[c] 'the sun,' *hwùi*,[d] 'an enclosure,' are produced; they may become the elements of complex characters. Thus *k'eù*[a] 'mouth,' after the addition of *hù*,[e] becomes *hù*,[f] 'to call out;' *jìn*,[b] 'man,' by the addition of *àr*,[g] 'you,' becomes *nì*,[h] 'you;' and *jì*,[c] 'the sun,' with *yŭ*,[i] 'the moon,' beside it, makes *mìng*,[k] 'bright,' and *hwùi*,[d] 'an enclosure,' with *wáng*,[l] 'a king,' placed within it, makes *kwŏ*, 'a kingdom,' the same as *kwŏ*.[m]

4. From this it will be seen that a Chinese character may consist of two parts, and that but one *syllable* is needed to express a complex character. These two parts are a "radical" and a "phonetic," the former conveys a fundamental notion to the whole character, and the latter indicates the sound by which it is expressed. But although it may be stated that the *radical* generally conveys something of its own meaning to the compound, and that the remaining part of the character is *phonetic*, this is not a constant rule. These facts only help the me

[a]口 [b]人 [c]日 [d]口 [e]乎 [f]呼 [g]尔 [h]你 [i]月
[k]明 [l]王 [m]國

mory when they take place, and we cannot say more for them: experience will shew their use. In the above examples, hu^e is phonetic in $h\bar{u},^f$ and $\dot{q}r^g$ was formerly called ni, and is therefore phonetic in $ni.^h$ The 'sun' and 'moon' unite to form bright or 'brightness'; but here is no phonetic: both parts are radicals.

5. The number of different characters in Chinese is upwards of 40,000, but many thousands of these are ancient forms, and therefore obsolete. Thousands more are simply curious variations of characters which are in use, but which are not wanted. Not more than 10,000, it is believed, enter into ordinary use, and 5000 are quite sufficient for the general purposes of literary composition.

6. Every character stands for an idea, and is expressed by a syllable. In as far, therefore, as it is seen *written*, it may constitute a word; but when its name is uttered—that is, when the syllable which expresses that character is *spoken*—the syllable means nothing. This may seem paradoxical, but it is nevertheless true, as will be found when practical explanation is given further on.

7. To express 40,000 characters, the Chinese have but about 500 syllables, which, when modified

in pronunciation, do not amount to more than 1200 or 1300 distinguishable syllables. Hence there must be, on an average, thirty characters to one syllable. And even if the number of characters be reduced to 5000, still it is clear that several characters must have a common name; and how is it possible to know what is intended when the same monosyllable has several meanings? It is impossible, unless the hearer is cognisant of the circumstances under which the monosyllable is spoken, and therefore readily divines the meaning thereof; or unless the monosyllable form a direct reply, as, *shí,* 'yes,' *pǔ,* 'not,'—' no,' for then it is clear. Chinese is commonly called a monosyllabic tongue, although it is quite impossible to make one's self intelligible in China by monosyllables. Let the best Chinese scholar try to translate the following line, without reference to the written character, and unless he can *guess* what the signification is, or obtain it by a sort of exhaustive process, he will fail: *Chi kwei chi ma chi yung,* or *ming fu mung chin tau chau.* The meaning does not appear, and is not conveyed, by these syllables themselves, apart from their proper connexion. If the *characters* for which they stand were known,

or the *connexion* and the *relation* of each syllable
to its neighbour were indicated, the sense of the
whole would be manifest. But the Chinese only
utter sounds—the doubtful expressions for characters
—and they employ no inflexions to show the mutual
relations of words: if, therefore, Chinese syllables do
not cohere to form words and phrases, and to make
polysyllables, Chinese is no language at all,—and this
amounts to a *reductio ad absurdum.* Monosyllables
in Chinese are meaningless; therefore Chinese is not
a monosyllabic language (if indeed there exists such
anywhere), and we are compelled to acknowledge
that English is far more of such a character than
Chinese. English may be spoken in monosyllables
—Chinese cannot. Thus: 'He went to the wood
and shot a hare, which he brought home in a bag,
and ate in a pie that night.' The truth is, that all
languages had only monosyllables to begin with.
All Hebrew roots are monosyllables, and all San-
skrit roots are monosyllables. The difference between Chinese and these ancient languages in this respect is this, that Chinese has, *by its written symbols,*
preserved the syllables of which it is composed distinct from each other, and has kept their meanings
also distinct generally. For nearly all Chinese

syllables have a distinct meaning still attaching to them, while some other languages contain many syllables, the meaning of which is lost, and which serve now for terminations, formatives, and particles, in those languages.

7. There are, however, means existing by which these monosyllabic representatives of the characters are wrought into intelligible language. They may be so connected with each other, and so intoned or accented, that we find some cohering, some nearly vanishing, others making themselves heard more clearly, and conforming themselves to the laws of euphony and the conditions of all human speech; and to such a degree does this cohesion, intonation, and accentuation of syllables take place, that, if the mother tongue of any Chinese were written down from his mouth, with appropriate signs, marking the emphasis and intonation which he produced, and making those syllables coalesce (or nearly so) which he uttered rapidly together, we should find that our production was a polysyllabic tongue—yea, very polysyllabic. Every thing depends on accent and emphasis to make a language polysyllabic. Without accent and emphasis, polysyllables become monosyllables. For instance, the passage, "*I re mem ber*

Sir with a me lan cho ly plea sure the si tu a tion of the ho nou ra ble gen tle man" (Burke), would, when thus dissected, read as Chinese is supposed to be read, with each syllable isolated and apart from the others.

8. But, by a process similar to that in use in all languages—by a natural arrangement, and of necessity—Chinese syllables cohere, and form polysyllables. Nouns, verbs, and particles are formed by the juxta-position and cohesion of syllables, all of which are sometimes significant. Sometimes one of the syllables is merely *formative*, like *er* in *butcher*, *ed* in *wounded, ing* in *singing*, or *ly* in *truly*.

9. With 5000 significant syllables, it may easily be conceived that many tens of thousands of words of two and three syllables are formed. The Chinese language is inexhaustible in its power of development in this way, and compound words are formed with great facility.

10. Of great importance is it, in the first place, to understand clearly the system of orthography for these Chinese syllables, and the qualities of the intonations which are attached to them: and in the next place, to learn a good many words of two syllables, independent of the characters which they express.

11. The Syntax of the Chinese language is simple and natural; but the proper adornment of the sentence by particles is more difficult. All that the reader of this little book may expect to find here is, directions how to acquire the spoken language,—common, more or less, to all China,—which is commonly called the Mandarin Dialect. The author's object has been to make this a stepping-stone to further efforts and a practical grammar of the first principles of Chinese Etymology and Syntax.

12. Only a few Chinese characters have been used here, not because it is unimportant to acquire a knowledge of them, but in order to leave the student at liberty to acquire the colloquial style, without, in the first instance, being kept back by having to attend to the characters which belong to each expression.

13. The author recommends the student to learn thoroughly the *Radicals*, as a first step. Until this is done he will labour unprofitably at complex characters. After the Radicals he will do well to master the *Formatives*, the *Appositives*, and the *Auxiliary Verbs*.

CHAPTER I.

ETYMOLOGY.

Section I.—ANGLO-CHINESE ORTHOGRAPHY.

1. The Roman alphabet will be employed in this work to express the Chinese syllables and words. The simple vowels employed are *a, i, u,* which are pronounced *ah, ee, oo,* as the vowels in *father, feet, rule.* Their simple combinations are, (1) *ai, au;* (2) *ia, iu;* (3) *ua, ui. Ai* and *au* are modified into *e* and *o,* pronounced *ay* and *ō,* as in *hay* and *note. Ia* and *iu* may be spelt *ya* and *yu;* and *ua* and *ui* may be spelt *wa* and *wi.* Other modifications of *ai* and *au* may be indicated by *ạ* and *ọ,* for the sounds of *a* 'in *organ* and *o* in *order. O,* when not final, or when affected by the short tone, does not need the dot, but must be pronounced as if it were written with the dot—*ọ. Iu* or *yu* may be modified by being pronounced as the French *u:* it will then be represented by *ü.*

Unions of these vowels may take place; thus, we may have *iai, iau, uai, uau, eu, ei, ea, oi, ou, üi, üa,* but all these are not required in the Mandarin.

The short vowels always correspond in form to the long vowels, from which they are distinguished by the usual mark, thus : *ă, ĭ, ŭ, ĕ, ŏ, ŭ.*

The consonants are to be pronounced as in English, with the exception of the letter *j,* which will follow the French, and *w* will occasionally stand for the *v.*

2. Synopsis of Orthography, with illustrative words. Each letter has but one sound.

I. VOWELS AND THEIR COMBINATIONS.

a, ă, father, fa..	*ia, iă,* yard, Yankee.
i, ĭ, machine, bit.	*io, iŏ,* York, yonder.
u, ŭ, rule, bull	*iu, iŭ,* you, juchhe (Ger.)
e. ĕ, they, bet.	*ai,* aisle.
o, ŏ, no, not.	*au,* cow (*broad.*)
ạ, ặ, organ, but.	*ei,* pie.
ọ, ộ, order, not.	*eu,* e + u = eou (Fr.)
ü, ü̆, lu, peut-être (Fr.)	*oi,* voice.
ö, Göthe (Ger.)	*ui,* ruin.
ie, iĕ, yea, yesterday.	*üi,* feuille (Fr.)

II. CONSONANTAL COMBINATIONS.

ch,	church.	*ng*,	anger.
chw,	hatchway.	*nw*,	inward.
j,	jaune (Fr.)	*ny*,	can you.
dj,	gin, James.	*sh*,	shine.
ju or *jw*,	jouir (Fr.)	*shw*,	rash wish.
hi or *hy*,	nearly = *shi*.	*ts*,	wits, tsz = t + sz.
hü,	nearly = *shü*	*tw*,	twist.
ki or *ky*,	nearly = *chi* = *ci* (Ital.	*tsw*,	Cotswold.
	and Pol.)		
kü,	nearly = *chü*.	*s*,	kiss.
kw	queen.	*z*,	squeeze.
lw	bulwark.	*sz*,	s + z.

SECTION II.—THE CHINESE "TONES."

3. Every Chinese syllable is distinguished by one of four or five intonations. The pronunciation of a character is called by a native its *shĭng-yĭn*,[ab] *shĭng*[a] meaning the *tone*, and *yĭn*[b] the *syllable*. The syllables may be formed and represented by the Roman letters, and the *tones* may be shewn by the following accents: ¯ ` ´ ˘, with the addition of

[a]聲 [b]音

dots, thus : ` ´ ˘ , where more than five tones are found.

4. There are in the Mandarin dialect five tones :—

    1st, *p'íng-shīng,*[a] 'even tone.'
    2d, *shàng-shīng,*[b] 'rising tone.'
    3d, *k'ü-shīng,*[c] 'departing tone.'
    4th, *jĭ-shīng,*[d] 'entering tone.'
    5th, *hiá-p'íng-shīng,*[ea] 'lower even tone.'

They are commonly called by the Chinese, *p'íng,*[a] *shàng,*[b] *kü,*[c] *jĭ,*[d] and in some dialects there are two series, *shàng,*[b] 'upper,' and *hiá,*[e] 'lower.' The Chinese do not generally indicate the "tones" in writing; but whenever they wish to mark the tone of a character, they affix a slight curve or hook to the corner of it. Each character is supposed to stand in a square, and the left-hand corner below is considered the first; the left-hand above, the second; the right above, the third; and the right-hand below, the fourth corner. These places correspond to the places for marking the tones.

5. These Chinese tones are simple modulations of the voice, such as are common to all languages;

    [a] 平 [b] 上 [c] 去 [d] 入 [e] 下

the difference being, that in Chinese they are defined and fixed to certain words, while in other languages they vary with the feelings of the speaker,
or the circumstances under which he speaks. Thus,
the sound or tone of voice in which Richard the
Third may be supposed to have shouted, "A horse! a
horse!" or as one would cry, "Fire! fire!" or a
master simply calling his servant, "John," corresponds with the first tone (*p'ing-shing*) of the
Chinese.

6. The fifth tone corresponds to the tone of a
categorical reply, ("yes," or "no,") as uttered
by a criminal at the bar, when answering, without
surprise or indignation, on being asked a question.
This limitation is necessary; for, if he replied "yes,"
with surprise, as if he meant further, "certainly,
but what then?" it would exemplify the second
"or rising tone" (*shàng-shing*), while the former
"yes" of simple assent, exemplifies the fifth or
"lower even tone" (*hià-p'ing-shing*).

7. The third or 'departing tone' (*k'ü-shing*) is
the tone of dramatic scorn or reproach, "Hence!"
"away!" "avaunt!" "what!" a tone of *nonchalance*,
or of forlorn hope, as in "No! all is lost!"

8. The following passage will, it is believed, aid

the student in realizing what the Chinese tones
are :—

> PORTIA. *Come,*[1] *merchant,*[5] have you any thing
> to *say ?*[2]
>
> ANTONIO. But *little ;*[5] I am *armed*[5] and well
> *prepared.*[5]
>
> Give me your *hand,*[1] *Bassanio ;*[5] fare you *well !*[3]
>
> *Merchant of Venice,* Act iv. Sc. 1.*

It should be particularly remembered that the
p'ing (‾) is a " calling " or " exclaiming " tone ;
the *shàng* (ˋ) is a " questioning " tone ; the *k'ù* (ˊ)
is a " despairing " tone ; and the *hià-p'ing* (ˆ) an
" assenting " tone ; the *jĭ-shīng* is an abrupt stop.

9. Twenty-five changes or permutations in the
relative positions of the five tones are possible, and
the student should accustom himself to read syllables, or words of two syllables, which have the
same tones, or the same tones consecutively. The
following list of words will do for practice in reading
the tones. Observe that four examples are given of
the sequences in tone ; thus :— - -, -ˏ, -ˌ, - ˏ, -ˏ, &c.

---

* The numerals affixed refer to the tones.

1. *weī-fūng*, 'dignity.'   *kūng-fū*, 'work.'
   chûng-sīn, 'center.'   *kō-kō*, 'elder brother.'

2. *gǎn-tièn*, 'favour.'   *shān-k͑ eù*, 'a mountain pass.'
   tūng-nǜ, 'a virgin.'   *ch͑wāng-k͑eù*, 'a window.'

3. *sūng-shǔ́*, 'a fir-tree.'   *kūng-heú*, 'a nobleman.'
   sāng-i, 'trade, business.'   *yiū-mǎn*, 'sorrow.'

4. *yīng-shǐ*, 'limestone.'   *ī-fǔ*, 'clothes.'
   sāng-jǐ, 'birth-day.'   *kīn-jǐ*, 'to-day.'

5. *sīn-ch͑ ǎng*, 'the heart.'   *fī-k͑iaû*, 'a drawbridge.'
   chaū-p͑ aî, 'a sign-board.'   *kūng-laû*, 'merit.'

6. *mà-fū*, 'a groom.'   *kiaù-ǎr*, 'a waiter, a valet.'
   siaù-sīn, 'attention.'   *liàng-sīn*, 'conscience.'

7. *chàng-tsᶎ*, 'the eldest son.'   *chǜ-tsᶎ*, 'the master.'
   k͑iaù-sheù, 'an adept.'   *shwǜi-sheù*, 'a sailor.'

8. *siè-tsᶎ*, 'to write.' (Gen.)   *paì-chíng*, 'to arrange.'
   tseù-sháng, 'to walk up.'   *paù-tsín*, 'to walk in.'

9. *kì-tě*, 'to remember.'   *kiaì-fǎ*, 'explanation.'
   niù-jǔ, 'beef.'

10. *k͑iuèn jín*, 'to advise people.'   *nǜ ǎr*, 'a girl.'
   tièn-ǎr, 'a little.'   *chì-t͑eû*, 'a finger.'

11. *hwā kŭng,* 'a painter.' *k'iaŭ-fŭ,* 'sedan-bearer.
    heŭ-sāng, 'a youth.' *tién-kiā,* 'a shopkeeper.'

12. *chău-k'i̇̀,* 'to stand up.' *kwó-tsì̇̀,* 'a fruit.'
    paŭ-sheŭ, 'a gunner.' *shéu-tsì̇̀,* 'a fan.'

13. *shé-tsŭ̈i,* 'to pardon.' *wán-kién,* 'to hear of.'
    k'aŭ-chú, 'to rely upon.' *k'ai-hú,* 'beggars.'

14. *shŭ̈i-chŏ,* 'to go to sleep.' *tá-mĕ,* 'wheat'
    kién-shwŏ, 'gossip.' *wán-tă,* 'dialogue.'

15. *hwá-ặr,* 'a word.' *paŭ-jín,* 'a reporter.'
    fú-jĭn, 'a woman.' *tá-hwáng,* 'rhubarb.'

16. *chŭ-sāng,* 'domestic *tŭ-shŭ̄,* 'to read aloud.'
    animals.'
    kiŏ-kặn, 'the heel.' *mŭ-hwā,* 'wood-shavings.'

17. *tŏ-sheŭ,* 'to snatch out *tsŏ-chŭ̀,* 'to act as
    of the hand.' master.'
    tĕ-sheŭ, 'to be successful.' *k̇ĭ-kwó,* 'to bear fruit.'

18. *shwŏ-tíng,* 'to decide.' *kwŏ-tú,* 'a kingdom.'
    k'è-k'í, 'etiquette.' *fă-sán,* 'to scatter.'

    tsŏ-jĭ, 'yesterday.' *yŭ̈-fă,* 'so much the more.'
    tsĭ-kĕ, 'immediately.' *k̇ĭ-yŏ,* 'to take medicine.'

20. *hiŏ-fâng,* 'a school-room.' *shwŏ-míng,* 'to explain,
    to apologize.'
    tĕ-laí, 'come on purpose.' *shĭ-t'eú,* 'the tongue.'

21. *ts'úng-sīn,* 'afresh.' *jú-kīn,* 'at present, now.'
    niên-kặng, 'age' (of a *nặng-kān,* 'power.'
    person).

22. *siuên-chuèn,* 'to revolve.' *ní-t'ù,* 'earth, soil, mud.'
    ch'ặng-twàn, 'length.' *wặn-lĭ,* 'style of good
    composition.'

23. *míng-fặn,* 'share, duty.' *süí-pién,* 'as you please.'
    yúng-í, 'easy.' *yuên-shwaí,* 'commander-
    in-chief.'

24. *hô-mŭ,* 'peace,' opp. *nân-tĕ,* 'hard to obtain.'
    'war.'
    fâng-ŭ, 'a house.' *wặn-yŏ,* 'a written contract.'

25. *yên-mô,* 'to grind.' *süí-ts'úng,* 'to follow.'
    hwüï-laí, 'to return.' *híng-ch'uên,* 'to sail about.'

SECTION III.—THE CHINESE CHARACTERS.

10. The elementary characters are the "Radicals,"
called by the Chinese *tsź-pú.* They are 214 in
number, and stand to the Chinese language in the
relation of an alphabet of forms, in place of an

alphabet of sounds. They represent, too, the fundamental notions which must be conveyed by all
human speech. The following list of their meanings will show their generic character, and serve
as a test-table for the student.

11. Classified synopsis of the meanings of the
tsź-pú :—

Parts of bodies.—Body, corpse, head, hair, down,
whiskers, face, eye, ear, nose, mouth, teeth, tusk,
tongue, hand, heart, foot, hide, leather, skin, wings,
feathers, blood, flesh, talons, horn, bones.

Zoological.—Man, woman, child; horse, sheep,
tiger, dog, ox, hog, hog's head, deer; tortoise,
dragon, reptile, mouse, toad; birds, fowls; fish;
insect.

Botanical.—Herb, grain, rice, wheat, millet,
hemp, leeks, melon, pulse, bamboo, sacrificial herbs;
wood, branch, sprout, petal.

Mineral.—Metal, stone, gems, salt, earth.

Meteorological.—Rain, wind, fire, water, icicle,
vapour, sound; sun, moon, evening, time.

Utensils.—A chest, a measure, a mortar, spoon,
knife, bench, couch, clothes, crockery, tiles, dishes,
napkin, net, plough, vase, tripod, boat, carriage,

pencil; bow, halberd, arrow, dart, axe, musical base, reed, drum, seal.

Qualities.—Colour, black, white, yellow, azure, carnation, sombre-colour; high, long, sweet, square, large, small, slender, old, fragrant, acrid, perverse, base, opposed.

Actions.—To enter, to follow, to walk slowly, to arrive at, to stride, to walk, to reach to, to touch, to stop, to fly, to overspread, to envelope, to encircle, to establish, to overshadow, to adjust, to distinguish, to divine, to see, to eat, to speak, to kill, to fight, to oppose, to stop, to embroider, to owe, to compare, to imitate, to bring forth, to use, to promulge.

Parts of the world and dwellings; figures; miscellaneous.— A desert, cave, field, den, mound, hill, valley, rivulet, cliff, retreat. A city, roof, gate, door, portico. One, two, eight, ten, eleven. An inch, a mile. Without, not, false. A scholar, a statesman, letters; art, wealth, motion; self, myself, father; a point; wine; silk; joined hands; a long journey; print of a bear's foot; a surname, a piece of cloth.

12. LIST OF THE "RADICALS."

Note.—The words in brackets (as *left*, *below*, *various*, &c.) are intended to show in what part of the complex character the radical may be looked for; *com.* means that the radical is a *common* word in use; *obs.* means that it is *obsolete* as a word; an asterisk denotes that the radical as such is of *frequent* use, and often found in complex characters. The radicals are arranged according to the number of strokes with which they are formed.

Radicals of *One* stroke.

1.   一   *yĭ*,* 'one,' 'the same' (various).

2.   丨   *kwăn*, 'perpendicular' (obs.) (through).

3.   丶   *chŭ*, 'a point' (obs.) (top and within).

4.   丿   *pĭ*, 'a curve' (obs.)

5.   乙   *yĭ*, 'a crooked line' 'one' in comp. 乚 (obs.)(top and left, right and through.)

6.   亅   *kŭ*,'a hooked stroke' (obs.) (through).

Radicals of *Two* strokes.

7.   二   *ăr*, 'two' (com.) (encloses, above, below).

齒 龍 龜 龠

214.

黃 黍 黑 黹 黽 鼎 鼓 鼠 鼻 齊

鬥 鬯 鬲 鬼 魚 鳥 鹵 鹿 麥 麻

頁 風 飛 食 首 香 馬 骨 高 髟

隶 隹 雨 青 非 面 革 韋 韭 音

辰 辵 邑 酉 釆 里 金 長 門 阜

豆 豕 豸 貝 赤 走 足 身 車 辛

160　　170　　180　　190　　200　　210

10	20	30	40	50	60	70	80	90	100	110	120	130	140	150	160	170	180	190	200	210	214
一	入	匕	囗	寸	干	心	无	比	片	用	矢	缶	臣	虍	豆	辰	隶	頁	鬥	黃	齒
丨	八	匚	土	小	幺	戈	日	毛	牙	田	石	网	自	虫	豕	辵	隹	風	鬯	黍	龍
丶	冂	匸	士	尢	广	戶	曰	氏	牛	疋	示	羊	至	血	豸	邑	雨	飛	鬲	黑	龜
丿	冖	十	夂	尸	廴	手	月	气	犬	疒	禸	羽	臼	行	貝	酉	青	食	鬼	黹	龠
乙	冫	卜	夊	屮	廾	支	木	水	玄	癶	禾	老	舌	衣	赤	釆	非	首	魚	黽	
亅	几	卩	夕	山	弋	攴	欠	火	玉	白	穴	而	舛	襾	走	里	面	香	鳥	鼎	
二	凵	厂	大	巛	弓	文	止	爪	瓜	皮	立	耒	舟	見	足	金	革	馬	鹵	鼓	
亠	刀	厶	女	工	彐	斗	歹	父	瓦	皿	竹	耳	艮	角	身	長	韋	骨	鹿	鼠	
人	力	又	子	己	彡	斤	殳	爻	甘	目	米	聿	色	言	車	門	韭	高	麥	鼻	
儿	勹	口	宀	巾	彳	方	毋	爿	生	矛	糸	肉	艸	谷	辛	阜	音	髟	麻	齊	

8. 丄 *teŭ,* (no sig. can be given of this (obs.) (above.)

9. 人 *jin,** contr. 亻 'a man' (com.) (above, left.)

10. 儿 *jin,* 'a man walking' (obs.) (below.)

11. 入 *jĭ,* 'to enter' (com.) (above).

12. 八 *pă,* 'eight' (com.) (below.)

13. 冂 *kiŭng,* 'a desert' (obs.) (encloses).

14. 冖 *mĭ,* 'to cover' (obs.) (above).

15. 冫 *pĭng,** 'an icicle' (obs.) (left) = 冰

16. 几 *kĭ,* 'a table, a bench' (encloses, right, below.)

17. 凵 *kăn,* 'a receptacle' (obs.) (encloses).

18. 刀 *taŭ,** contr. 刂 'a knife' (com.) (below, right).

19. 力 *lĭ,** 'strength' (com.) (below, right).

20. 勹 *paŭ,* 'to wrap up' (obs.) (encloses).

21. 匕 *pĭ,* 'a spoon' (obs.) (right).

22. 匚 *făng,* 'a chest' (obs.) (encloses).

23. 匸 *hĭ.* ' to hide ' (obs.) (encloses).

24. 十 *shĭ,* ' ten ' (com.) (various, below).

25. 卜 *pŭ,* ' to divine ' (obs.) (above, right).

26. 卩 *toĭ* or 㔾 ' a seal ' (obs.) (right).

27. 厂 *hăn,* ' a shelter ' (obs.) (hangs over).

28. 厶 *meŭ,* ' crooked ' (obs.) (above).

29. 又 *yiŭ,* ' the hand,' ' again ' (com.) (right, below).

Radicals of *Three* strokes.

30. 口 *k'eŭ,** ' a mouth ' (com.) (left, below).

31. 囗 *hwĭĭ,* ' an enclosure ' (obs.) (encloses).

32. 土 *t'ŭ,** ' earth, soil ' (com.) (left, under).

33. 士 *sĭ,* ' a scholar ' ' a statesman ' (com.) (above, right).

34. 夂 *chĭ,* ' to follow ' (obs.) (above).

35. 夊 *shŭĭ,* ' to walk slowly ' (obs.) (below).

36. 夕 *sĭ,* ' evening ' (com.) (various).

37. 大 *tá,** ' great ' (com.) (above or below).

38.　女　*nù,** 'woman' (com.) (left, below) 攵.

39.　子　*tsz̀,** 'a son' (com.) (below, left).

40.　宀　*miēn,** 'a roof' (obs.) (above).

41.　寸　*ts'ǎn,* 'an inch' (com.) (right, below).

42.　小　*siaù,* 'small' (com.) (various).

43.　尢　or 兀　or 尤　*wǎng* or *yiù,* 'more' (obs.) (left).

44.　尸　*shī,* 'a corpse' (com.) (above).

45.　屮　*ch'ě,* 'a sprout' (obs.) (above).

46.　山　*shān,* 'a mountain' (com.) (left, above).

47.　川　or 巛 *ch'uēn,* 'a stream' (com.) (various).

48.　工　*kūng,* 'work' (com.) (various).

49.　己　*kì,* 'self' (com.) (below).

50.　巾　*kīn,** 'a napkin' (com.) (left, below).

51.　干　*kān,* 'a shield' (com.) (various.)

52.　幺　*yaū,* 'young' (obs.) (left, doubled).

53.　广　*yěn,** 'a covering' (obs.) (covers).

54. 及 *yīng*, 'a long journey' (obs.) (left).

55. 廾 *kŭng*, 'folded hands' (obs.) (below).

56. 弋 *yĭ*, 'a dart' (obs.) (right).

57. 弓 *kūng*,* 'a bow' (com.) (left, below).

58. 彐 or 彑 *ki*, 'a pig's head' (obs.) (above).

59. 彡 *shăn*, 'long hair' (right).

60. 彳 *chĭ*,* 'to walk' (obs.) (left).

Radicals of *Four* strokes.

61. 心 *sīn*,* contr. 忄 'the heart' (com.) (below).

62. 戈 *kŏ*,* 'a spear' (com.) (right).

63. 戶 *hú*, 'a one-leaved door,' 'a family' (com.) (above).

64. 手 *sheŭ*,* contr. 扌 'the hand' (com.) (left, below).

65. 支 *chī*, 'a branch' (com.) (right).

66. 攴 *pŭ*,* contr. 攵, 'to touch' (right).

67. 文 *wǎn,* contr. 攵, 'to paint letters' (com.) (below).

68. 斗 *teù,* 'a dry measure,' 'the North Star' (com.) (right).

69. 斤 *kīn,* 'an axe,' 'a Chinese pound' (com.) (right).

70. 方 *fāng,* 'a square, a place' (com.) (left).

71. 无 *wú,* in comp. 旡, 'wanting, not.'

72. 日 *jǐ,** 'the sun,' 'a day' (com.) (left, and elsewhere).

71. 曰 *yǔ,** 'to speak' (com.) (below, and elsewhere).

74. 月 *yü,** 'the moon, a month' (com.) (left).

75. 木 *mǔ,** 'wood' (com.) (left, below).

76. 欠 *k'ién,** 'to owe, to want' (right).

77. 止 *chì,* 'to stop at a point' (com.) various).

78. 歹 *taì,** 'a rotten bone,' 'bad, putrid' (com.) (left).

79. 殳 *shu,* 'to kill' (right).

80. 毋 *wŭ,* 'not, without' (com.) (below).

81. 比 *pĭ,* 'to compare' (com.) (various).

82. 毛 *maŭ,** 'hair (not human), fur, feathers' (com.) (left).

83. 氏 *shĭ,* 'a family' (com.).

84. 乞 *k'ĭ,* 'vapour' (obs.) (right, above).

85. 水 *shwuĭ,** contr. 冫, 'water' (com.) (left, below).

86. 火 *hŏ,** contr. 灬, 'fire' (com.) (below, left).

87. 爪 *chaŭ,* contr. 爫 , 'claws' (com.) (above).

88. 父 *fŭ,* ' a father,' (com.) (above).

89. 爻 *hiáu,* 'to imitate' (left).

90. 爿 *chwáng,* 'a couch' (obs.) (left).

91. 片 *pién,* 'a splinter' (left).

92. 牙 *yá,* 'molar teeth' (com.) (left).

93. 牛 *niŭ,** contr. 牜, 'an ox' (left, below).

94. 犬 *k'iuèn,* contr. 犭, 'a dog' (com.) (left).

Radicals of *Five* strokes.

95. (Sheet I. 5) *hiŭen*, 'colour of the sky, dark' (com.) (combined).

96. 王 *yŭ*,* 'a jewel' (com.) (left).

97. 瓜 *kwā*, 'fruit of the melon kind' (com.) (right or left).

98. 瓦 *wà*, 'tiles, bricks' (com.) (right, below).

99. 甘 *kān*, 'sweet' (com.).

100. 生 *sāng*, 'to be born, to live' (com.).

101. 用 *yúng*, 'to use' (com.) (combined).

102. 田 *t'ién*, 'a field' (com.) (left, below).

103. 疋 *p'ĭ*, 'a piece of cloth' 'a foot' (com.) (below).

104. 疒 *nĭ*,* 'disease' (obs.) (left).

105. 癶 *pŭ*, 'to stride' (above).

106. 白 *pĕ*, 'white, clear' (com.) (left, above).

107. 皮 *p'ĭ*, 'skin, bark' (com.) (right, left, below).

108. 皿 *mìng,** 'dishes' (com.) (below).

109. 目 *mŭ,** 'the eye' (com.) (left, or contr. above).

110. 矛 *meŭ,* 'a barbed spear' (left).

111. 矢 *shì,* 'an arrow' (left).

112. 石 *shĭ,** 'stone, rock' (com.) (left, below).

113. 示 *shì,** contr. 礻 or 示 'an omen from heaven' (com.) (left, below).

114. 禸 *jeù,* 'the print of an animal's foot, a trace' (obs.) (below).

115. 禾 *hó,** 'grain' (com.) (left).

116. 穴 *hiŭ,* 'a cave, a hole' (com.) (above).

117. 立 *lĭ,* 'to stand, to establish' (com.) (left).

Radicals of *Six* strokes.

118. 竹 *chŭ,** contr. ⺮, 'bamboo' (com.) (above).

119. 米 *mì,** 'rice (uncooked)' (com.) (left).

120. 糸 *mì,** also written 系 and 絲, 'raw silk (threads)' (com.) (left, below).

121. 缶 *feŭ*, 'an earthenware vase' (left).

122.   *wàng*, contr. 罒 , 冋, and 冗, as in 罕 'a net' (above.) (See sheet I. 1.)

123. 羊 *yáng*, 'a sheep' (com.) (left, above).

124. 羽 *yŭ*, 'wings' (com.) (various :—above, below, right).

125. 耂 *laŭ*, 'old' (com.) (above); contr. into in ¹ and ².

126. 而 *ạr*, 'whiskers;' 'and, yet' (com.).

127. 耒 *lŭi*, 'a plough-handle' (left).

128. 耳 *ạr*,* 'the ear' (com.) (left, below).

129. 聿 *yŭ*, 'a pencil' (left and below).

130. 肉 *jŭ*,* contr.   , 'flesh' (com.) (left, below).

131. 臣 *chīn*, 'a subject; a statesman' (com.) (left).

132. 自 *tsź*, 'self; from' (com.) (various.)

133. 至 *chí*, 'to come to' (com.) (below, and elsewhere).

---

¹ *k'au*, 'aged,' com. 'to examine.'   ² *chè*, 'this, he who,' &c.

134. 臼　*k'iù*, 'a mortar' (various).　(Sheet I. 2.)

135. 舌　*shǐ*, 'the tongue' (com.) (left).

136. 舛　*chu'èn*, 'to turn the back on' (obs.)

137. 舟　*cheū*, 'a boat' (com.) (left).

138. 艮　*kǎn*, 'disobedient; limits' (right).

139. 色　*sǐ*, 'colour; appearance' (com.) (right).

140. 屮屮　*tsaù*,* contr. ⺾, 'grass; plants' (com.) (above).

141. 虍　*hù*, 'a tiger' (obs.) (above).

142. 虫　*chúng*,* 'an insect; a reptile' (com.) (left, below).

143. 血　*hiǔ*, 'blood' (com.) (left).

144. 行　*híng*, 'to walk; to do' (com.) (encloses).

145. 衣　*ī*,* contr. 衤, 'clothing, covering' (com.) (left, below).

146. 襾　*yā*, also written 西¹, 'to cover over' (obs.) (above).

¹ properly pronounced *sī*, 'the west.'

Radicals of *Seven* strokes,

147   見   *kién,** 'to see' (com.) (right, below).

148.   角   *kiŏ,* 'a horn; a corner' (com.) (left, below).

149.   言   *yen,** 'words; to speak' (com.) (left, below).

150.   谷   *kŭ,* 'a valley' (left).

151.   豆   *teù,* 'a wooden sacrificial vessel; beans' (below, left).

152.   豕   *chì,* 'a pig' (left or below).

153.   豸   *chì,* 'reptiles' (left).

154.   貝   *péi,* 'a pearl shell' (com.) (left, below).

155.   赤   *chì,* 'flesh colour' (com.) (left).

156.   走   *tseù,** 'to walk, to run' (com.) (left)

157.   足   *tsŭ,** contr. ⻊ or ⻊, 'the foot, enough' (com) (left, below).

158.   身   *shīn,* 'the body; trunk' (com.) (left).

159.   車   *kü* or *chĕ,** 'a carriage' (com.) (left).

160.   辛   *sīn,* 'bitter,' H.C. (com.) (doubled, right).

161. 辰 *shin,* 'time ; an hour,' H.C. (com.) (various).

162. 辵 *chŏ,** contr. 辶 , 'motion' (obs.) (left).

163. 邑 *yĭ,** contr. 阝, 'a city' (com.) (right).

164. 酉 *yiŭ,* ' new wine ' (com.) (left).

165. 釆 *piĕn,* 'to distinguish' (left).

166. 里 *lĭ,* 'a Chinese mile ; a village' (com.) (below).

Radicals of *Eight* strokes.

167. 金 *kīn,** ' gold, metal ' (com.) (left).

168. 長 *ch'áng,* contr. 镸, 'long, old ' (com.)

169. 門 *măn,** ' a door ' (com.) (encloses).

170. 阜 *feŭ,** contr. 阝, ' an artificial mound of earth (left).

171. 隶 *tai,* ' to reach to ' (right).

172. 隹 *chuĭ,** ' short-tailed birds ' (right).

173. 雨 *yü,** ' rain ' (com.) (contr. form above).

174. 青 *tsíng,* 'azure, sky-blue' (com.) (left).

175. 非 *fî,* 'not so, false' (com.).

Radicals of *Nine* strokes.

176. 面 *mién,* 'the face' (com.) (left).

177. 革 *kĕ,* 'untanned hide, without hair' (com.)

178. 韋 *weì,* 'tanned hide' (left).

179. 韭 *kiù,* 'leeks' (various).

180. 音 *yīn,* 'sound, tone' (com.).

181. 頁 *yĕ,** 'the head' (com.) (right).

182. 風 *fūng,* 'wind' (com.) (left).

183. 飛 *fî,* 'to fly' (com.).

184. 食 *shĭ,** contr. 𩙿, 'to eat' (com.) (contr. form on the left).

185. 首 *sheù,* 'the head; the chief' (com.).

186. 香 *hiāng,* 'fragrance' (com.).

Radicals of *Ten* strokes.

187. 馬 *mà,** 'a horse' (com.) (left, below).

D

188. 骨 *kŭ*, 'a bone' (com.) (left).

189. 高 *kaŭ*, 'high' (com.).

190. 髟 *piaŭ*, 'long hair' (above).

191. 鬥 *teú*, 'to fight' (obs.) (encloses).

192. 鬯 *chǎng*, 'fragrant plants' (below).

193. 鬲 *lĭ*, 'a tripod with crooked feet' (left, below)

194. 鬼 *kwei*, 'a departed spirit, a ghost' (com.) (left).

Radicals of *Eleven* strokes.

195. 魚 *yŭ*, 'a fish' (com.) (left).

196. 鳥 *niaù*, 'a bird' (com.) (right).

197. 鹵 *lù*, 'salt' (left.)

198. 鹿 *lŭ*, 'a stag' (com.) (above).

199. 麥 *mĕ*, 'wheat' (com.) (left).

200. 麻 *má*, 'hemp' (com.) (above).

Radicals of *Twelve* strokes.

201. 黃 *hwǎng*, 'yellow, colour of earth' (com.) (left).

202. 黍 *shü*, ' millet ' (com.) (left).

203. 黑 *hĕ*, ' black ' (com.) (left, below).

204. 黹 *chî*, ' to sew, to embroider ' (left).

Radicals of *Thirteen* strokes.

205. 黽 *mùng*, ' a frog ' (com.) (below).

206. 鼎 *tíng*, ' a tripod ' (com.).

207. 鼓 *kù*, ' a drum ' (com.) (above).

208. 鼠 *shù* a rat ' (com.) (left).

Radicals of *Fourteen* strokes.

209. 鼻 *pí*, ' the nose ' (com.) (left).

210. 齊 *ts'î*, ' to adjust, to adorn ' (com.) (above).

Radical of *Fifteen* strokes.

211. 齒 *chî*, ' front teeth ' (com.) (left).

Radicals of *Sixteen* strokes.

212. 龍 *lúng*, ' a dragon ' (com.).

213. 龜 *kwêi*, ' a tortoise ' (com.).

Radical of *Seventeen* strokes.

214.　龠　*yŏ* ' a flute with three holes' (left).

The student will do well to refer to the sheet of Radicals.

13. AN ALPHABETIC ARRANGEMENT OF THE RADICALS, BY WHICH THE NUMBER OF EACH MAY BE READILY FOUND.

ár, 7, 126, 128.

ch'áng, 168, 192.

chau, 87.

che, 159.

ch'ĕ, 45.

cheu, 137.

chī, 34, 65, 77, 133, 153, 204, 211.

chĭ, 60, 155.

chin, 131.

chŏ, 162.

chu, 3.

chŭ, 118.

ch'uen, 47, 136.

chüi, 172.

chang, 142.

chwang, 90.

fang, 22, 70.

feu, 121, 170.

fi, 175, 183.

fu, 88.

fung, 182.

han, 27.

hĕ, 203.

hi, 23.

hìang, 186.

hìau, 89.

hing, 144.

hìü, 116, 143.

hiuen, 95.

ho, 86, 115.

hu, 63, 141.

hwang, 201.

hwüi, 31.

i, 145.

jeu, 114.

jĭ, 11, 72.

jin, 9, 10.

jŭ, 130.

kan, 17, 51, 99.

kạn, 138.

kau, 189.

kĕ, 177.

k'eù, 30.

ki, 16, 49, 58, 84.

kien, 76, 147.

kin, 50, 69, 167.

kiŏ, 148.

k'iu, 134, 179.

k'iuen, 94.

kiung, 13.

ko, 62.

kü, 159.

kǔ, 6.

kù, 207.

kǔ, 150, 188.

kūng, 48, 55, 57.

kwā, 97.

kwạn, 2.

kweī, 194, 213.

laù, 125.

lè, 166,

lǐ, 19, 193, 117.

lù, 197.

lǔ, 198.

lùi, 127.

lûng, 212.

mà, 187, 200.

mạn, 169.

maù, 82.

mě, 199.

meū, 28, 110.

mè, 119.

mǐ, 14.

miěn, 40, 176.

mìng, 103.

mǔ, 75, 109.

mùng, 205.

nǐ, 104.

niaù, 196.

niú, 93.

nù, 38.

pǎ, 12.

paū, 20.

pě, 106.

péi, 154.

pè, 21, 81, 107, 209.

pǐ, 4, 103.

piaū, 190.

piěn, 91, 165.

pīng, 15.

pǔ, 25, 66, 105.

sāng, 100.

shān, 46, 59.

sheù, 64, 185.

shī, 44, 83, 111, 113, 152.

shǐ, 24, 112, 135, 184.

shīn, 158, 161.

shü, 79, 202, 208.

shuī, 35.

shwuè, 85.

sǐ, 36, 139.

siaù, 42.

sīn, 61, 160.

sz, 28, 33, 120.

tá, 37.

taè, 78, 171.

taū, 18.

teû, 8, 68, 151, 191.

t'iên, 102.

tìng, 206.

tsạn, 41.

tsaù, 140.

tseù, 156.

ts'ǐ, 210.

tsǐ, 26.

tsîng, 174.

tsǔ, 157.

tsè, 39, 132.

t'ù, 32.

wà, 98.

wăn, 67.	yaŭ, 52.	yiŭ, 29, 43, 164.
wăng, 43, 96, 122.	yĕ, 181.	yŏ, 214.
weĭ, 178.	yĕn, 53, 149.	yŭ, 124, 173, 195.
wŭ, 71, 80.	yĭ, 1, 5, 56, 163.	yŭ, 73, 74.
yâ, 92, 146.	yĭn, 180.	yŭ, 129, 96.
wâng, 123.	ying, 54.	yŭng, 101.

Section IV.—ON READING AND WRITING THE CHARACTERS.

14. Chinese is written or printed in columns, and is read from the top of the page down each column, beginning with that on the right hand. Marks of punctuation or accentuation are sometimes used, but not always. They are merely a point to indicate the parts of a sentence, or a curve at the corner of a character, to show that a change of intonation is required. A large circle ◯ appears sometimes at the beginning of a paragraph to mark the commencement of a new subject. Black dots, commas, or small circles, are occasionally placed at the side of characters to show that such contain a remarkable sentiment. In classical compositions these marks are generally omitted, as the well-read scholar is

supposed to be able to discern the proper divisions of the sentence from the particles in it.

15. The characters are written with a hair pencil, which is held in an upright position, quite vertical, between the second and third fingers. The ink used is that commonly called "Indian ink," which may be prepared by rubbing it with water upon slate or some other hard material. The paper should not be glazed much, but be such as will absorb the ink readily.

16. The strokes or marks required in Chinese writing, and with which the characters are made up, are the following. They should be made by a single stroke of the pencil.

(1) The *point* (*tién* or *chù*) ⟍ or ⟊ or

(2) The *horizontal* (*hwǎ*) ⎯ (3) The *perpen-dicular* (*chǐ*) | (4) The *hook* (*keù*) ⏌ (5) The *spike* (*tiaù*) ⟋ (6) The *sweep* (*p'iě*) ⟋ (7) The *dash* (*pǎ*) ⟍ (8) The *angle* (*kǜ*) ⅂ .

These strokes appear in the following characters, which the student will do well to copy frequently, until he can write them well.

氵 川 二 刁 氺 口

氺 永 衣 養

17. It is of great importance to know the order in which the strokes of the characters should be made, as this often supplies a clue to reading the cursive forms in which the strokes are combined very strangely. The full and all the cursive forms of Chinese characters are used in Japanese, and they form the groundwork of the Japanese syllabary: hence the advantage of correctly writing them.

The following simple rules will be of assistance :—

1. Begin either at the top or on the left-hand side. 2. When a perpindicular or dash cuts a horizontal line or one leg of an angle, the latter are to be written first, (cf. radicals 19, 24, 29, 32, 33, 41, 43, &c.) 3. An angle at the top on the right side is made with one stroke, and unless *pǐ* (rad. 4.) or *kwạn* (rad. 2.) is affixed to the left of

it, the angle is made first. In radicals 18, 19, 26, 39, 39, 44, 49, 105, 124, 129, 178, 183, it is made first. In radicals 13, 20, 34, 35, 36, 76, 122, 130, the angle is made second. 4. An angle at the bottom on the left is also made with one stroke, if it be alone, or be joined to a perpendicular on the right, leaving the top or right side open, (cf. radicals 17, 22, 23, 28, 38, 45, 46, 49, 90, 206.) The characters in which *wu* (80, five strokes) occurs, are exceptions to this rule; the angle on the left is made first; then the angle on the right; the points, next; and the horizontal last. 5. The angles ⁷ and ᴸ in 門 *mǎn* 'a door' are made first on each side respectively. 6. Horizontal lines precede perpendiculars, when these cross each other; but should the perpendicular terminate with the base line, then the base line is final. 7. In such characters as the radicals 42, 85, 77, 141, 197, 204, 211, the perpendiculars above, or in the middle of the symbol, are made first. 8. In such characters as *k'eù* 口 'mouth' (rad. 30.) the perpendicular on the left is to be written first; and the interior of such characters as 國, 固, and 四, 圍, is filled up before the base line is written.

Section V.—ON THE PARTS OF SPEECH.

18. Though Chinese monosyllables cannot be placed in any grammatical category, so as to remain therein and be used constantly in one form, and with the same force in the sentence, words may be found which have such grammatical value, and which may be parts of speech, and remain such.

The position also of a syllable or word may determine what part of speech it is, while the same syllable, disconnected from the sentence or phrase, would have no grammatical worth at all.

A system, therefore, of word-building, and a set of rules respecting the positions of words in the sentence, will form the basis of Chinese Grammar, at least so far as the determination of the grammatical value and classification of words is concerned. The syntax of clauses requires separate consideration.

19. Chinese words may be divided into *nouns,* (*i.e.* substantives or adjectives) *verbs,* and *particles.* Nouns may be distinguished by their form when certain *formative particles* are present as affixes. The meanings of their component syllables will also assist. There are from three to ten com-

monly understood significations to one syllable; if the word be of two syllables, the student will have to eliminate several meanings, and rest in those which mutually correspond. Thus, one syllable of a word will limit another and determine the part of speech: take hing and wei: *hing* 行 may mean *to walk, to do, to punish, fortunate,* &c., and *wei,* 爲 may mean *dignity, to do, to become,* &c.; but when they are united in one word, hing-wei, we must take the meanings which are common to both, to *make* or *do,* and the word recognised is the noun ' actions.' Here synonymes are united to form a noun. This is often the case, and when some progress has been made in the written characters and their radical meanings, it will be interesting to see the etymology of such compounds; but for all practical purposes, at which only this little book aims, it is sufficient to accept the words given in the vocabulary, and to use them according to the directions.

20. The following general principles of word-building, both for nouns and verbs, may be found useful :——

1. *Synonymes* are united to strengthen each other's meaning.

2. *Extremes* in meaning are united to form general or abstract terms.

3. The syllables are *in construction*, the former having the position and force of the genitive case.

4. The syllables are *in apposition*, being explanatory of each other, though not synonymous.

EXAMPLES.

(1) *yèn-mŭ,* ' the eye;' *chūng-sīn,* the centre;' *mŭ-wì,* ' the end.'

(2) *hiūng-tí,* ' brethren;' *tō-shaù,* ' quantity.'

(3) *shíng-jín,* ' a sage;' *k'ù-niên,* ' last year.'

(4) *kĕ-jín,* ' a guest;' *Chi Hwang-tí,* ' the Emperor Chi;' *Wạn-wang,* ' King Wạn.'

These principles are found to hold in respect of verbs as well as nouns.

Section VI.—ON NOUNS.

21. Nouns may be considered as (1) *primitive,* (2) *derivative,* or (3) *composite.* By primitive nouns in Chinese we may understand monosyllables, which are used in their original signifi-

cation. By derivative nouns, such as are derived
from primitives, by the addition of a formative
syllable, and become dissyllables with a distinct
meaning. By composite nouns are intended such as
are compounded of primitives, and in which the
original meanings of the component syllables are
retained and combined to form a new meaning.

EXAMPLES.

(1) *fán* 'rice;' *fūng,* 'wind;' *wặn,* 'letters or
literature;' *mà,* 'horse.'

(2) *wặn-ặr,* 'a writing;' *mà-fū,* 'a groom.'

(3) *wặn-lì,* 'style' (in writings); *mà-pĭ,* 'horses'
paŭ-fūng, 'a gale.'

22. Primitive nouns are rarely used in the
relations expressed by the oblique cases. They
generally unite with some other syllable to form a
new word, *e. g.* while we say 'the smell of rice,'
the Chinese would say, 'rice-smell,' *i.e. fán-hiáng,*
not *fán-tĭ hiang.* 'The force of the wind' would
be 'the wind-force,' *i. e. fūng-lĭ,* which, like *fặn-
hiáng* is one word—a composite noun.

23. A primitive noun can seldom mean any
thing when standing alone. It needs an adjunct

of some kind, or to be in construction as the subject or object of a sentence. The whole then often becomes a phrase, and may be treated as one long word.

EXAMPLES.

haù-fán, 'good rice;' *fán-haù kĭ* (*chĭ*), 'rice is good to eat;' *paû-fŭng,* 'fierce wind, a gale;' *fŭng-nĭ-tĭ,* 'the wind is contrary;' *yĭ-wán-ch'á,* 'a cup of tea;' *ch'á jĭ,* 'the tea is hot.'

By this means, *fán,* 'rice,' is distinguished from *fán,* 'to offend against;' *fŭng,* 'wind,' from *fŭng,* 'a needle,' and *ch'á,* 'tea,' from *ch'á* 'a raft.'

24. Derivative nouns are formed by adding the following syllables, as *formatives,* to primitive roots. The order shows their comparative frequency of use. Examples will be found in the vocabularies and exercises.

1. *tsż* 子 'a son;' as *siáng-tsż,* 'a box,' *taū-tsż,* 'a knife.'

2. *ąr* 兒 'a child;' as *míng-ąr,* 'a name,' *tsiŏ-ąr,* 'a bird, a sparrow.'

This is very commonly used for this purpose

in the Peking dialect, in which it appears in many connections to form words. (*cf. Wade's* Hsin tsing-luh.)

3. *fŭ* 夫 'a fellow, a person;' as *nŭng-fŭ*, 'a husbandman;' *kiaŭ-fŭ*, 'a sedan-bearer.'

4. *sheù* 手 'a hand,' 'a person;' as, *shwŭĕ-sheù*, 'a sailor;' *hŭng-sheù*, 'a murderer.'

5. *jín* 人 'man;' as, *k'ĕ-jín*, 'a guest.'

6. *nŭ* 女 'woman;' as, *tûng-nŭ*, 'a virgin.'

7. *tsiāng* 匠 'an artisan;' as, *mŭ-tsiāng*, 'a carpenter;' *t'iĕ-tsiāng*, 'a blacksmith.'

8. *kūng* 工 'a workman;' as, *páng-kŭng*, 'a day-labourer.'

9. *kweī* 塊 'a clod, a lump.

10. *t'eû* 頭 'a head, a round mass;' *jĭ-t'eû*, 'the sun;' *kŭ-t'eû*, 'a bone.'

11. *sāng* 生 'a production, a person;' *chŭ-sāng*, 'cattle;' *siēn-sāng*, 'a teacher.'

12. *sź* 師 , or, *sz-fú*, 'a teacher;' *t'í t'eû sź-fú*, 'a barber.'

13. *kiā* 家 'a family, a person;' *jin-kiā,* 'a person;' *tŭng-kia,* 'the master.'

14. *hŭ* 戶 'a house, a person.'

15. *chŭ,* 主 'a lord;' *ch'uĕn-chŭ,* 'the captain of a ship.'

16. *sheù* 首 'a chief;' *hwŭi-sheù,* 'the chief of a society,' 'a President.'

17. *ti* 帝 'a ruler,' as, *hwâng-ti,* 'emperor.'

18. *k'i* 氣 'breath, feeling;' *nú-k'i,* 'anger;' *t'ú-k'i,* 'exhalations.'

19. *fŭng* 風 'wind, air, manner;' *wei-fŭng,* 'dignity;' *wăn-fŭng,* 'literary taste.'

20. *sing* 性 'nature, disposition, faculty;' as, *kì-sing,* 'memory.'

25. Composite, or compound nouns, are formed in various ways. Their component syllables bear the following relations to each other :—(1) The *appositional;* (2) the *genitival;* (3) the *datival;* and (4) the *antithetical.*

26. By the *appositional* relation between the

syllables of a word, the student will perceive what is meant when he considers the words, *statute-law, pear-tree, crab-fish, flock of sheep,* (*i. e.* sheep-flock) in his own language. Here one syllable explains the other, and means the same thing; the syllables are in *apposition.*

But this apposition may vary. The syllables may hold the following relations: they may be, (1) a *repetition,* (2) *synonymes,* (3) *specific and generic terms,* (4) the *commencement of a series,* (*cf.* the *A, B, C.*)

Examples.

(1) *nai-nai,* 'lady;' *kō-kō,* 'elder brother, sir.'

(2) *chūng-kiĕn,* 'the midst;' *ni-t'u* 'soil, or mud; híng-weí,* 'actions;' *shwŏ-hwá,* 'talk.'

(3) *lĭ-yŭ,* 'the carp;' *sūng-shü,* 'the fir-tree,' (*cf.* Art. 27.)

(4) *kiă-tsĭ,* 'the cycle;' *kŭng-heú,* 'a nobleman;' the five titles of nobility being *kûng, heú, pĕ, tsĭ, nan.*

27. Under the head of apposition comes also an important class of syllables, which have been variously denominated *classifiers, classitives,* and

numerals. But none of these terms seem quite appropriate, and the designation *appositive* is here applied to them, as being more in accordance with the part which they play in compounds. In English we say, *a flock of sheep, a glass of wine, a gust of wind*; but in some languages—German for instance— we have, *ein glass wein, ein stück brod.* The words are in apposition. The Chinese noun, whether primitive or derivative, requires one such syllable, appropriate to its signification, to stand in apposition, as it were, and to form and embody the whole word. This syllable is the generic term, while its associate is the specific name.

The common appositives, with their associated terms, are the following :—

1. *kó* 個 with *man* and *things,*

2. *chĕ* 隻 with *animals, ships,* &c., things that can move.

3. *kién* 件 with *affairs, clothes,* &c.

4. *k'wei* 塊 with *dollars* and things in *lumps,* or of *irregular shape; e. g. yĭ-kwei-tĭ,* 'a piece of land.'

5. *t'iaŭ* 條 with *long* things, as *roads, rods, spears,* &c.; *e. g. yĭ t'iaŭ-lú,* 'a road, a piece of land.'

6. *ṛà* 把 with things which have *handles,* as *knives; e. g. yĭ pà-taŭ,* 'a knife.'

7. *tsó* 座 with objects *resting* in a place, as *houses, sedans; e. g. yĭ tsó-fâng-tsż,* 'a house.'

8. *pạn* 本 with *volumes* of books; *e. g. yĭ pạn-shū,* 'a book.'

9. *kạn* 根 with *trees* and things which may be planted in the ground; *e. g. yĭ kạn-shü-mŭ,* 'a tree.'

10. *chāng* 張 with things *spread out,* as *paper, tables; e. g. yĭ chī-chāng,* 'a sheet of paper.'

11. *chī* 枝 with things like branches; *e. g. yĭ chī-hwā,* 'a flower.'

12. *ṛ'ĭ* 匹 with *horses* (properly a *pair*); *e.g. yĭ pĭ-mà,* 'a horse.'

13. *tüi* 對 with things which go in *pairs,* as *shoes; e.g. yĭ tüi-hiaŭ,* 'a pair of shoes.'

14. *shwāng* 雙 with things that go in *pairs*—a *brace*.

15. *kiĕn*   問 with *buildings*; e. g. *yĭ kiĕn ŭ*, 'a house.'

16. *fūng*   封 with things *sealed*, as *letters*; e g. *yĭ fūng-sín* 'a letter.'

When these appositives come after the nouns to which they are attached, the two syllables form a general term; e. g. *mà-pĭ*, 'horses;' *ch'uĕn-chĕ*, 'ships.' Appositives always belong to the noun itself, and not to the numeral.

28. Under the genitival relation are such compounds as are formed by the former of the two syllables being in that relation to the latter; e. g. *lŭ-kiŏ*, 'stags' horns;' *mŭ hwā*, 'wood-flowers = shavings;' *shān-k'cù*, 'mountain-pass;' *mà-ch'áng*, 'horses'-place = stable-yard;' *chén-ch'áng*, 'fighting-arena = battle-field.'

Composite nouns with a *genitival* relation existing between their component syllables are such as have the first syllable attributive to the second, as when a genitive case or a participle precedes in European languages, *e. g.*

T'iĕn-chŭ, ' heaven's Lord '=' God', this is used
  by the Roman Catholics only for *God.*
t'iĕn-k'ĭ, ' heaven's breath '=' weather.'
niù-jŭ, ' ox-flesh '=' beef.'

29. Composite nouns, with the first of their
component syllables in the *datival* relation to the
other, are formed variously; with nouns or with
verbs, the latter as participles; *e g.*

hiŏ-fáng, ' a room *for* learning '=' schoolroom.'
píng-lĭ, ' law *for* soldiers '=' discipline.'
yín-k'ú, ' a storehouse *for* silver '=' treasury.'

Composite nouns are also formed by syllables of
opposite signification   Such are nouns which express abstract notions and general ideas; *e. g.*

hiūng-tí, ' elder and younger brother'=' brethren.'
k'îng-chúng, ' lightness and heaviness '=' weight.'
tŏ-shaù, ' muchness and fewness '=' quantity.'

30. It has been common to consider certain
words in Chinese as adjectives, and others as nouns,
but it is more correct to regard both these kinds
of words as belonging to but one class. They are
nouns substanstive; *e. g. tá* is ' greatness,' and not
' great' simply; *fú* is ' richness,' and not merely

'rich.' When we say *tá-jín*, 'great man, your excellency,' these syllables form but *one* word. When *tï*, the genitive particle, appears between two syllables, they may be held to be two words— nouns in construction; and when it is omitted the two syllables form a compound : just as *house-hold, life-boat, fox-hound, dove-cote*. Even when *tï* is used after a verb it forms a substantive ; *e. g.* hiŏ-*tï*, 'a learner; *ché-kó fâng tsẕ tá-tï*, 'this house (is) a large one ;' without *tï*, 'this house (is) large.'

Chī 之 in the book-style, and ˙*chè* 者 per- form the same task as *tï* 的 in giving the force of *one, an individual*, and by imparting unity and strength to the phrase.

Section VII.—ON NUMBER, GENDER, AND CASE OF NOUNS.

31. The Chinese seem to consider the bare word as indicative of plurality or generality, for they distinguish the *plural* only in extraordinary cases, and where it is absolutely necessary to do so ; but they constantly mark the *singular*, which is itself a proof that the simple word modified is plural in meaning.

32. To define clearly the singular, *yǐ* or *yǐ-kó*, 'one,' must be used before the noun with the appositive ; *e. g. yǐ-kó-jín*, 'a man ;' *yǐ chě-ch'uên*, 'a ship.' The plural is exactly denoted in several ways :

(1) By *repeating* the syllable in certain words, as *jǐ-jǐ*, 'every day ;' *jín-jín*, 'every man.'

(2) By *prefixing* one of the following syllables which mean 'all' or 'many' :—*chung* 衆, *chū* 諸, *tō* 多, *hǔ-tō* 許|, or *haù-tō* 好|, *shǐ* 庶, *fán* 凡, *sǐ* 悉.

(3) By *appending* one of the following syllables which also signify 'all,' *kiaī* 皆, *t'ū* 都, *k'ū* 俱, *hiěn* 咸, *kǔ* 舉, *tǎng* 等, *peī* 輩, *tsīuen* 全, *mǎn* 們, *tsí* 儕, *tsien* 僉.

Some of these are more commonly used than others. It should be observed, too, that they nearly all refer to the plural of designations of men and not of animals or objects in general. For the latter the apposition placed after the name gives the plural notion.

(4) When a numeral above *one* is used it is unnecessary to denote the plural in any other way than by that numeral which is used; *e. g. sān jín,* 'three men;' *sź chĕ-mò,* 'four horses.'

(5) Many idiomatic phrases convey a plural sense, and indicate a *class* of persons or a *whole,* *e. g.*

sź-haì, 'the four seas'='the whole world.'
pĕ-kwān, 'the 100 officers'='the mandarins.'
lŭ-fâng, 'the six rooms'='the whole government,' 'the six councils of state.'
wán-mín, 'the 10,000 people'='all the people.'
kiù-cheŭ, 'the nine islands'='the whole world.'

33 The *genders* of nouns are rarely expressed; but when there is a necessity for such distinction a syllable is prefixed or suffixed to the name of the animal; *e. g.*

(1) *năn,* 'male,' *nŭ,* 'female,' (pref.) *fú,* 'father,' *mù,* 'mother,' *tsź,* 'son,' *nŭ,* 'daughter,' (suff.) for names of *men and women.*

(2) *kŭng,* 公 or *meú,* 'male,' *mù,* 毑 'female,' (pref.) for names of *quadrupeds;* and

(3) *hîung* 'male,' or *tsź,* 'female,' (pref.) for names of *birds.*

34. The relations usually expressed by *cases* are shown in Chinese by the presence of certain *particles* (pref. or suff.) or by *position.* Thus, *tĭ* 的 (suff.) is the mark of the *genitive* case; *pĭ, kĭ,* or *yŭ* 彼, 給, 與 (pref.) shows the dative; the *accusative* is indicated by the position of the word immediately *after* the verb; *yā* or *ā* 呀 (suff.) marks the *vocative*; *ts‘ûng,* 從 (pref.), 'to follow, —from,' with *lai,* 來 (suffix) 'to come,' mark the *ablative; e. g. ts‘ûng Pĕking lai,* 'from Peking;' *yúng,* 用 or *ĭ,* 以 'to use,' (pref.), serve to form the *instrumental* case; and *tsai* 在 (pref.), 'in,' forms the *locative; t‘ûng,* 同 'together with' (pref.)=*cum,* and it is the expression of an *ablative* sometimes.

Certain of these particles only go with persons; *e. g. t‘ûng;* but *yúng* and *ĭ* are of general use, though they are employed more particularly in speaking of materials; *e. g. t‘ûng yĭ-kó-jĭn,* 'with a man,' but *yúng yĭ-pà-taū,* 'with a sword or knife.'

The following paradigms will be useful.—
Shanghai tĭ, 'of or belonging to Shanghai.'

taú Shanghai lai, 'to Shanghai.'

ts'úng Shanghai lai, 'from Shanghai.'

tsaí Shanghai, 'in Shanghai.'

tsúng Shanghai kwó-k'ü, '(passed) through Shang-hai.'

pĭng-tĭng, 'soldiers,' *pĭng-tĭng tĭ,* 'of soldiers.'

yĭ-kó pĭng-tĭng, 'a soldier,' *kó pĭng-tĭng,* 'the soldier.'

yĭ-kó pĭng-tĭng tĭ, 'a soldier's' *kó pĭng-tĭng-tĭ* 'the soldier's.'

pĭ yĭ-kó pĭng-tĭng, 'to, or by a soldier.'

tĭ yĭ-kó-pĭng-tĭng, 'for (instead of) a soldier.'

t'úng (or *hó*) *yĭ-kó pĭng-tĭng,* 'with a soldier.'

yúng (or *kiaŭ*) *yĭ-kó-pĭng-tĭng,* 'by means of a soldier.'

Section VIII.—ON COMPARISON.

35. The usual method is to *compare* two objects by using the word *pĭ,* 比 'to compare.' Thus, *nĭ pĭ ngó tá-tĭ,* 'you, compared with me, are great, (properly, 'belonging to greatness'). And in the books, *yü* 於 is employed in nearly the same way. Thus, *tsè jín tá yü ngó,* 'this man is greater than I.'

But the following particles are prefixed to qualifying nouns to increase the force of the comparison and to intensify the meaning; *e. g.*

(1) *kăng,* 更 'more;' *kiă,* 加 'to add;' *yiú,* 又 'again;' *tsai,* 再 'more, again;' *hwân,* 還 'still more;' *yŭ,* 越 'to pass over;' *yŭ,* 愈 'to exceed.'

(2) *ting,* 頂 'the top;' *kĭ,* 極 'the extreme point;' *haù,* 好 'good;' *t'ai,* 太 'great, very;' *shĭn,* 甚 or *tsúi,* 最 'very;' *tsŭ.* 絕 'to cut off;' *hặn,* 恨 'to hate;' *shĭ-fặn,* 十分 'ten parts.'

Section IX.—ON THE PRONOUNS.

The pronouns in Chinese are very numerous. Some are used only in the *books,* others only in *conversation.* The following list will show the pronouns of the different persons :—

Pers.	in Books.		in Conversation.	
Sing.				
1st,	*wù,* 吾 *yú,* 余 or *yû,* 予		*ngò* or *wò,* 我 ·	
2d,	*jù* 汝 or *ặr,* 爾		*nì* or *nì-nă,* 你納 ·	
3d,	*k'ĭ,* 其 or *î,* 伊		*t'ā,* 他 ·	

36. The plural of the classical or book pronouns is formed by adding thereto generally *tẳng* 等, but various other syllables, indicative of plurality, are also employed. In colloquial compositions, *mận* 們 is added to form the plural; *e. g. ngỏ-mận,* ' we ;' *nỉ-mận,* ' you ;' *t'ả-mận,* ' they.'

37. The *cases* of pronouns are produced in the same way as the cases of nouns. The genitive case is formed by adding *ti* 的 to the pronoun ; *e. g. ngỏ-tỉ,* ' my ' or ' mine ;' *wỏ-mận-tỉ,* ' our ' or ' ours.'

38. The Chinese have no *possessive* pronouns distinguishable by forms : the genitive case must be used instead.

39. The *reflexive* pronoun is formed by *tsẻ* 自 , or *kỉ,* 已 ' self,' being added to the personal pronouns, and in the colloquial style both syllables are used ; *e. g. ngỏ-tsẻ-kỉ,* ' I myself.'

40. The *demonstrative* pronous are numerous, some of them being common to classic writings, others being confined to the colloquial style. Among the former are *k'i* 其 , *i* 伊 , *kử* 厥 , ' that ;' *tsẻ* 此, *shí* 是 ' this ;' and among the latter are *nă-ko* 那 个 ' that,' *ché-kó* 這 个 , ' this.'

41. The *interrogative* pronouns are also of two classes : such as are classical, and such as are colloquial. The classical are, *hŏ,* 何 'what?' *kĭ,* 豈 'how?' *shŭ,* 孰 'who?' *k'ĭ,* 幾 'how?' The colloquial are, *shŭĭ,* 誰 'who?' *nā-kó,* 那 'which?' *shin mó,* 甚 么 'what?' and *k'ĭ,* 'how many?'

42. A further list of common pronouns are, *meŭ,* 某 'a certain one;' *meī,* 每 'every;' *pĭ,* 別 'other;' *siè,* 些 'a little;' *kŏ,* 各 'each;' *sú,* 數 'several.'

43. The following are pronominal expressions :—
sŭĭ piĕn-shimmó, 隨 便 'whichever;' *ché-yáng-kó,* 樣 个 'this sort, such;' *pŭ-kwán-shimmó,* 'no matter what.'

44. Various honorific or contemptible terms are used for pronous. Among such substitutes are the following :—*kweī,* 貴 'noble;' *pí,* 敝 'vile;' *tá,* 大 'great;' *kaū,* 高 'high;' *tsūn,* 尊 'honourable;' *ts'ién,* 錢 'mean;' *shé,* 舍 'homely.'

SECTION X.—ON THE VERB.

45. The Chinese verb has no moods and tenses as such. But various syllables are added to it, by which its force is more exactly defined. These may have the force of verbs or be mere particles.

46. The simple and unaided verb in Chinese expresses the infinitive or imperative of other languages; *tseù,* 走 is either 'to walk,' 'the 'walking' or 'walk,' 'go!'

47. If *liaù,* 了 'to finish,' be added to *tseù, tseù-liaù* means 'it is walked,' or if a subject precedes, simply 'walked.'

48. By adding *kwo,* 過 'to pass over;' *wân,* 完 'to finish,' with or without *liaù* following the simple verb, the *past* tense is produced.

49. By putting *ī,* 已 'already;' *kí,* 死 'finished;' *tsâng,* 曾 'already done,' *before* the verb, the *past* tenses and the *past participle* are produced.

50. By placing *yaù,* 要 'to will,' *tsiāng,* 將 'to take,' or *tsiù,* 就 'to proceed to,' *before* the verb, the *future* tense and its variations are

formed; and *k'ŏ,* 可 or *tĕ,* 得 'can,' forms the *potential.*

51. Certain verbs come in as auxiliaries to verbs whose meanings are similar to their own. The following list of these will be useful:—

tĕ, 得 'to obtain;' *k'aī,* 開 'to open;' *ch'ŭ,* 出 'to come out;' *chŭ,* 住 'to rest in;' *laî,* 來 'to come;' *k'ŭ,* 去 'to go away;' *kién,* 見 'to see;' *chŏ,* 着 'to take effect.'

And these correspond to the separable prepositions in other tongues; *e. g.* to cut *out,* to run *away,* to sit *up,* to come *along,* to run *together,* &c.

52. The following are examples of tenses in Chinese:—

ngò kién-kwó-liaù t'ā, 'I have seen him.'

ngò yaú-kién-kwó t'ā, 'I wish to see him.'

t'ā tsiāng-yaú k'ŭ, 'he will go,' or 'he is about to go.'

t'ā tseù-kwó-laî-liaù, 'he has walked over.'

Other examples will be found in the dialogues.

SECTION XI.—ON THE SUBSTANTIVE VERBS.

53. An important class of verbs in Chinese is that

of the substantive verbs, which are variously used according to the logical relation of the subject and predicate in the sentence. Thus, *shi*, 是 'to be,' means 'is,' where the simple copula alone is required, the predicate being *natural* to the subject; *e g.* in 'fire is hot.' *Yiu*, 有 'to have,' means 'is' when the notion of the property having been *acquired* is intended; as in 'he is rich.' *Wei*, 爲 'to become,' means 'is' when the idea of *growth* or *change* is implied; as, 'he is a king,' (*i. e. now*, he was not so once). A similar usage attaches to *tsó*, 做 'to make, to do,' which is like the German *thun*, preserved in our present indicative, 'he does sit,' &c. *Tsai*, 在 'to be in a place,' is used for 'is' when *locality* enters into the idea conveyed by the phrase; *e. g.* in 'he is at home.'

54. These substantive verbs may be qualified and modified in their force by certain particles which signify *then*, *all*, *also*, &c., very much like the use of the German particles *ja*, *gar*, *auch*, *noch*, *doch*, in simple sentences. Such words are *tsui*, 最 'then,' *yà*, 也 'also,' *tū*, 都 'all'

55. Any verb may be formed into an attributive in the form of a participle by adding thereto *tĭ*, the genitive particle; and, consequently, any tense of a verb may be changed into the corresponding participle in the same way.

SECTION XII.—ON THE ADVERBS AND PARTICLES.

56. The Chinese language is very rich in adverbs, for any expression may be treated adverbially in certain positions in the sentence. But there are some words that are positively and clearly adverbs in form or meaning. Such are the following :—

1. ADVERBS OF TIME.

kīn-t'iĕn, ' to. day,' *tsŏ-t'iĕn,* ' yesterday.'

jŭ-kīn, ' now,' *míng-t'iĕn,* ' to-morrow.

siĕn-shí, ' beforetime,' *kù-shī,* ' formerly.'

pién-shí, ' then,' *tsiú-shí,* ' there.

ì-kīng, ' at present,' *mŭ-hiá,* ' just now.'

2. ADVERBS OF PLACE.

ché-lì, ' here,' *nā-lì,* ' there.'

tsaí-tsz̀-tí, ' in this place,' *tsai·nā-t'eŭ,* ' in that place.'

chŭ-chŭ, ' everywhere,' *kŏ-tí,* ' in every place.'

F

3. ADVERBS OF MANNER.

ché-yáng, ' in this way;' *yĭ-yáng,* ' in the same way.'

4. ADVERBS OF QUANTITY.

ché-yáng-tō, ' so much,' *t'ai-tō,* ' too much.'

5. ADVERBS OF QUALITY.

These are formed by uniting an adverb of manner to an adjective :—

ché-yáng-haù, ' so good.'

yĭ-yáng-haù, ' equally good.'

Particles which imply *intensity, frequency,* or *repetition,* are joined to adjectives to form adverbs ; as,

t'ai, 太 ' too,' *kwó,* 過 ' to exceed.'

6. AFFIRMATIVE VERBS.

shí, ' it is ' = ' yes,' *pŭ-shí,* ' it is not ' = ' no.'

kwó-jĕn, ' certainly,' *shĭ-tsai,* ' truly.'

The usual form of affirmative is to repeat the verb of the interrogative sentence ; thus,

nĭ yaú laĭ mò ? ' will you come ?'

yaú-laĭ, ' I will come ' = ' yes.'

The substantive verbs are used frequently as affirmative adverbs.

7. NEGATIVE ADVERBS.

The negative adverbs are *pŭ*, 不 'not,' *mŭ*, 沒 'without,' *fī*, 非 'not,' *mŏ*, 莫 'not, do not,' and some others.

8. ADVERBS OF DOUBT.

Such adverbs are the equivalents of *perhaps* and *perchance* : *e. g.*

hwŏ-chè, 或 者 'perhaps ;' *chĕ-p'á*, 只 怕 'I fear, I suppose,' 'perchance.'

9. INTERROGATIVE ADVERBS.

kì-shí, 幾 時 'when ?' *tsaí-nā-lì*, 在 那 裡 'where ?'

kì-t'sź, 幾 次 'how often ?' *kì-tō*, 幾 多 'how many ?'

57. The Chinese generally use verbs of appropriate signification for prepositions ; *e. g.*

taú, 到 'to reach to,' for 'to,' *Lat. ad.*

tsaí, 在 'to be in,' for 'in.' (See p. 64.)

ts'ŭng, 從 'to follow,' for 'from,' *Lat. per* or *de.*

hiáng, 向 'to go towards,' for 'towards.'

ì, 以 and *yúng,* 用 'to use,' for 'with, by;' *Lat. de, ex.*

hô, 和 'concord,' for 'with;' *Lat. cum.*

t'úng, 同 'the same,' for 'with' = *cum.*

yiú, 由 'origin,' for 'from;' *Lat. ex,*

taí, 代 'to act for,' for 'instead of;' *Lat. pro.*

58 Certain words are used in Chinese in regimen with the noun, to form the notion expressed by the preposition in some languages. Such are *niú,* 內 'interior;' *waí,* 外 'exterior;' *lì,* 裡 'interior;' *sháng,* 上 'superior;' *hiá,* 下 'inferior.' In construction they stand thus :—

> *tsaí-ch'ing-niú,* 'in the city.'
> *tsaí-ch'ing-waí,* 'outside the city.'
> *tsaí-mà-sháng,* 'on a horse.'
> *tsaí-leú-hiá,* 'below stairs.'

59. Conjunctions are rare in Chinese.   In the

classical books they are represented by verbs generally ; *e. g. kĭ,* 及 'to reach to ;' *píng,* 并 'to unite together ;' *liên,* 連 'to connect together ;' and a few others are used for *and, even,* etc.

60. The interjections in Chinese are numerous. They have various significations, and imply *surprise, admiration, interrogation,* or are mere *exclamations* or *euphonic* particles.

EXAMPLES.

ai-yā! 唉愛 呼 'ah!' *k'ŏ-liĕn!* 可 憐 'pity, have pity.'

kĭ-miaú!   'wonderful !'

mó at the end of a sentence denotes an interrogation which asks simply for information.

nĭ is an interrogative particle, which implies a state of doubt and uncertainty.

ā is often merely euphonic or exclamatory at the end of a clause.

PART II.

SYNTAX.

61. Chinese words are arranged in sentences, naturally and logically. The word which qualifies precedes that which it qualifies. The *position* of a word, therefore, determines its relative grammatical value. The presence of certain particles, too, defines the nature of some words and clauses.

62. The word which expresses the time *when* of an action usually stands first, and it is safest in composition to put the adverb of time *when* before all other words, unless it be a personal pronoun. Thus, *ming-t'iēn wǒ yaú laí,* or *wǒ ming-t'iēn yaú laí,* ' I shall come to-morrow ;' *wǒ-mǎn tiēn-t'iēn yaú chǐ-fán,* ' we must eat every day.'

63. The designation of *place* follows that of *time. t'ǎ-mǎn t'iēn-t'iēn tsaí Peking,* ' They are every

day in Peking; *shi-shi tsai Kwǎng-tūng tà-chǝn,* 'They are always fighting in Canton.'

64. The subject of a sentence always stands before its verb; but adverbial expressions of different kinds may come between.

65. The subject is often understood from the previous clause or from the circumstances.

66. The adjective, or word used as such, always precedes its noun. When a qualifying word follows a noun it is in the predicative form; *e. g.*

haù-jín, is a *good man,* (one word) but *jīn haù* is a complete sentence: 'this man is a good man.'

67. All attributive words and clauses precede. Hence the relative clause in English is to be turned into an attributive and placed before its antecedent noun (expressed or understood) in Chinese.

wǒ-kiaù-tǐ jín, 'the man whom I teach.'

68. The expression of *length, duration, height,* &c., is placed at the end of its clause; *e. g. hiǎ-yǜ sān-t'iēn,* 'it has rained for three days.'

69. The following general rules for the construction of nouns will be useful :—

(1) When two nouns come together the former

is in the genitive case, and it generally forms a compound word, as *horse-man*, &c., in English. The word for 'spring' (of the year) is *chặn-t iĕn*, 'spring's sky.'

(2) But two nouns may form an enumeration simply; *e. g. mà-yáng*, 'a horse and a sheep;' *jĭ-yŭ*, 'the sun and the moon.'

(3) Or one of the nouns may be in apposition to the other; *e. g. jín-kiā*, 'man-person, a person.'

(4) Or the former may be a subject of a sentence, and the latter the predicate; *e. g. fán haù*, 'the rice is good.' And here it may be remarked, that in reality such words as *haù*, 'good,' *tá*, 'great,' which we have occasionally called adjectives, are nouns, *haù*, meaning 'goodness,' *tá*, 'greatness.'

(5) Lastly, the latter of two nouns may be an adverbial expression, especially in classical style; *e. g. kiuèn yé sheú kiā*, 'the dog by night guards the house.'

Any other mode of construing two nouns in juxtaposition would render the sense absurd.

70. When a noun and a verb come together, the following rules may be observed:—

(1) The noun may precede and be the subject to the verb, or be an adverbial expression; *e. g.*

ngó shwŏ, 'I say ;' *mà-paù-tĭ* 'galloping like a horse.'

(2) The noun may follow and be the object of the verb, or be an adverbial expression ; *e. g.*

tà-fă-liaù yĭ-kó-jín, 'sent a man.'

71. The Chinese are fond of putting words in parallel and similar positions in the same sentence, and by antithesis or some other figure arranging the syllables of a clause ; *e. g.*

t'án-tiēn, shwŏ-tí, 'he discoursed of heaven and talked of earth '='he gossiped.'

tŭng-taù sī waī, 'it fell in the east, it fell in the west '='it fell in every direction.'

72. Repetition is very common in Chinese to express a *good many* or the *frequency* of an action ; *e. g. haù-haù súng ngó,* 'escort me forth very well '='conduct me properly.'

PART III.

EXERCISES AND DIALOGUES IN CHINESE.

1. SIMPLE PHRASES.

tsing-nì. ' if you please ;' *to siĕ,* ' many thanks.'

wó-yaú, ' I want ;' *pī-wó,* ' give to me.'

pŭ-yaú, ' do not ;' *shín-mó,* ' what ?'

pŭ-túng, ' I do not understand ;' *k'ó-ì,* ' it may be.'

tsiú-laí, ' then come '='I will come directly.'

tsìng-tsó, ' be seated.'

haù-yā? ' how do you do ?' or *nì-nă háù ?*

nì-nă yè haù mó ? ' are you well ?'

wó shwăng-kwaí, ' I am well.'

ché-lì-laí, ' come here.'

yaú shìn-mó? ' what do you want ?'

t'úng wó tseù, ' walk with me.'

pŭ tĕ-hiên, ' I have no time.'

yiù sź-ts'íng, ' I am busy.'

t'iĕn-k'í haù, ' the weather is fine.'

yaú kĭ fán, 'I want to eat rice'='I want my dinner.'

shí t'ā-tĭ, 'It is his.'

tsaí nâ-lì ? 'where is it?' or 'where is he?'

wŏ sāng-píng, 'I am unwell.'

nĭ shí shüí ? 'who are you?'

pŭ-yaú túng-sheù, 'do not move.'

nĭ-nă pŭ-yaú taú ché-lì laí, 'do not come here.'

kĭ-hiá-chŭng ? 'what o'clock is it?'

shínmó shí-heú ? 'what time is it?'

2. LONGER PHRASES.

tsìng-ī-sāng laí, haù pŭ-haù ? 'shall I call a doctor?'

sié-sié pŭ-yaú, 'no, thank you.'

nā-yĭ-kó ī-sāng kaū-míng-tĭ, 'that doctor has a great (high) reputation.'

yiù shínmó yuên-kú ? 'what reason is there?'

wŏ pŭ chī-taú, 'I do not know' (the fact).

wŏ pŭ-tŭng-tĕ, 'I do not understand' (the language).

wŏ pŭ jín-tĕ, 'I do not know' (the person).

mŭ-yiù lĭ-liâng, 'he has no strength.'

yiù tō-shaù yīn-tsz ? 'how much money have you?'

t'ā yiù pạn-sź, 'he has ability.'

kĭ-niên jín-tĕ t'ā ? 'how many years have you known him ?'

sän-niên tū jín-tĕ t'ā, ‘I have known him for three
   years ;’ or, *tū jín-tĕ t'ā sän-niĕn.*

nâ-lǐ kiĕn-kwó t'ā? ‘where did you see him ?’

tsai tsó-yǐ-tsó, ‘sit down again.’

wŏ fă-kiun liaù, ‘I am wearied.’

wŏ pǐ-tíng kwei-kiā, ‘I must return home.’

kiā tsai nâ-lǐ? ‘where is your home ?’

tsai Pĕkīng, ‘in Peking.’

nǐ tsai chìng-wai tsó shìmmo ? ‘what have you been
   doing out of the city ?’

yiù shi-hĕû tà-lǐ, ‘sometimes I hunt.’

yiù shi-hĕû tà-yǜ, ‘sometimes I fish.’

yiù shi-hĕû t'ŭ-shū, ‘sometimes I read.’

3. USEFUL PHRASES AND QUESTIONS.

ché-kó tūng-sī shīnmŏ yúng? ‘of what use is this ?’

ché-kó kiaū-tsó shìmmo? ‘what is this called ?’

shí nâ-lǐ lai-tǐ? ‘where does it come from ?’

ché-kó shìmmó kiā-tsiĕn? ‘what is the price of this ?’

Chūng-kwŏ hwá kǐ-kiù hiŏ-tĕ lai? ‘how long will it
   take to learn Chinese ?’

yǐ-niĕn k'ŏ hiŏ-tĕ, ‘in a year you may learn.’

tsìng nǐ-nă míng-t'iĕn laù wŏ-tǐ fâng-tsz̀ kǐ-fán, ‘I
   invite you to come to-morrow to my house to
   dine.’

t'ièn yaú hiá-yù, tsìng nì-nă tsié kó yù-sán, 'It is about to rain, please to lend me an umbrella.'

ché-tiaú-lú k'ŭ taú nâ-lì? 'where does this road go?'

pặn-niên ch'â-tsiú haù pǔ haù? 'is the tea-gathering good this year or not?'

ch'â-tsiú haù, ch'â fūng-shíng-tǐ, 'the harvest of tea is abundant.'

líng-sź-kwān chŭ t aí nâ-lì? 'where does the Consul live?'

yâng-ch'uên tsaí shímmó shí heú taú? 'when do the foreign ships arrive.'

meí-niên wù-lŭ yü chī kiên, 'every year, in the fifth or sixth month.'

hiên-tsaí wí-tsāng taú, 'they have not yet arrived.'

shé-hiá hwâ nyiù siē sź-tsíng yaú-pán, 'at home I have still a little business to do.'

tsź haú-ch'â, míng Li-ki, t'úng lŭ-pă ạr-shǐ siāng, 'this chop of tea is called *Li-ki*, and altogether contains 620 boxes.'

PART IV.

EXERCISES IN COLLOQUIAL CHINESE.

EXERCISE 1.

Words used in the following exercise :—
Pronouns *wò*, 'I,' or 'me,' or *nì-nă*, 'you,' *t'ā*,
' he :' add *mąn* to form the plural of pronouns.

to have, *yiù*.

to speak, *shwŏ*, or *kiàng*.

to give, *kĭ*, or *pī*.

to ask, to beg of, *k'iú*.

to beseech, *k'ąn-k'iú*.

to want,(fut.); *yaú*,'to will.'

to be able,can,may,(poten.)

   k'ŏ-ì, and *nâng-keú*.

to forget, *wáng, wáng-kì*.

to do, to act, *tsó*.

friend, *păng-yiú*.

a knife, *taū-tsż*.

to call, *kiaú*, (*chiaú*.)

to thank, *sié*.

what ? *shīmmo ?*

one, (of an affair) *yĭ kién*.

this, *ché-kó*.

that, *nâ-kó*.

gladly, *tsíng-yuên*.

to be polite, *chī-lì*.

to wish for, to want, *yuén-i*.

affair, something, *sż-tsíng*.

to depend on, *ī-kaú*,

to trouble, *tō-fán*.

formality, ceremony, *lĭ.*
freely, *fáng-sīn,* (lit. let go heart.)
to receive, *sheú.*
good, well, *haù.*
sir, *laù-yê.*
many, *tō, hū-tō.*
not, *pŭ.*

do not use, it is not necessary, *pŭ-pĭ.*
one (of a knife), *yĭ-pá.*
favour, *găn-tièn.*
very, *hăn* or *shĭ-făn.*
to like, to be pleased with, *hwān-hì.*
it is, or it was, yes, *shí.*

liaù, after a verb forms the past tense.

Translate into Chinese.

I have something to ask of you. What is it? Speak freely! I want you to give me a knife. Do this for me. I beseech you, Sir, to do me this favour. Gladly! Many thanks! Very well! If I receive your favour I shall never forget it. You are very polite! I am troubling you. What do you want? Do not use so much formality. I like you! It is not! You may depend upon me. What do you want me to do? Directly you speak I will act. Whatever you want I will do it.

Notes.—For '*what is it?*' say '*it is what?*' for '*directly*' and a verb, say '*one*' (*yĭ*) with the verb, placing the personal pronoun, if there is one, *first.*

The personal pronoun 'I' is frequently omitted in Chinese.

The negative precedes the verb, except when *liaù* or *tě,* 'can,' is added, then *pŭ,* 'not,' comes between *liaù* or *tě* and the principal verb. For '*what do you want me to do?*' say '*call me to do what?*'

EXERCISE 2.

Words to be used. The previous vocabulary must also be referred to, and it will be advisable occasionally to turn to the larger vocabulary at the end of this book.

to know how, *hwüí.*

middle kingdom, (China) *Chūng-kwŏ.*

language, to say, *hwá.*

mô, an initiatory particle used at the end of a general question.

tsūng, an intensifying particle = *indeed* ; (it must precede the phrase.)

not to have, or not (in questions), without, *mŭ-yiù.*

afterwards, *heú-laí.*

a certain person, *meú-jín.*

to tell, to inform, *kaú-sū.*

not· yet, have not yet, *wí-tsáng.*

if you please, *tsìng-nì.*

to hear, *t'ing-kién.*

to listen, to obey, *t'ing.*

to come, *lai.*

at a distance from, *li * * * yuèn.*

can say, *shwŏ-tĕ.*

cannot say, *shwŏ-pŭ-tĕ.*

what I say, *wò sò-shwŏ.*

what I said, *wò sò-shwŏ-liaù.*

sò, means ' that which.'

tū, or *ts'iuĕn,* before an expression adds force = all, perfectly, completely.

to see, *kién.*

to forget, *wăng-kì.*

to be clear about, *mîng-pĕ.*

why? *wei shimmó.*

to reply to, *tă-yíng.*

clearly, *ts'īng-ts'ú* or *ts'ūng.*

a little, *yĭ-tièn-ắr.*

can understand, *tûng-tĕ*; to ask, *wăn.*

here, *ché-lì*; there, *nā-lì.*

meaning, *i-sź.*

to explain, *kiaī (chaì)*; to explain, *kiaì-shwò.*

consequence, *kwăn-hī.*

suppose, *pī-făng.*

to think, *sź-siàng.*

G

so, *ché-yáng*.
to know, *jìn-tĕ*.
how many times? *kì-t'sĕ*?
to remember, *kì tĕ*.
to forget, *wáng-kì*.

Do you know how to speak the Chinese language? Did you speak? I have not yet indeed
heard that. A certain man told me. Afterwards
I told him. Did you say this or not? If you
please, what is this? *or,* Allow me to ask what this
is. Do you know this? I can say; I cannot say.
What! do you not reply?—Do you hear what I
say? I cannot hear. Speak a little more distinctly.
Come here and listen. At a distance from that
man, I cannot hear what he says. Do you understand clearly what he says? Do you understand
what he said? What I said, did you quite understand? What you said I perfectly understood. I
quite understood. I did not understand at all.
Were you clear about it or not? What is the
meaning of this? How do you explain it? Suppose I do not understand, what would be the consequence? I only think this is so.—Do you know
him? How many times have you seen him? I do

not remember the number of times. Have you forgotten me? I cannot recollect distinctly.

The rule about *pŭ* ('not') coming between the verb and its auxiliary holds in *t'íng-kién* and many other compound verbs.

The simple copula verb *to be* is often omitted.

The demonstrative pronouns are only used emphatically.

EXERCISE 3.

Words to be used.

day, *t'iēn*.	fine, *haù*.
sun, *jĭ-t'eŭ*.	cloudy, *yŭn-tsai*.
a while, *yĭ-hwúĭ*.	stars, *sīng-sŭ*.
eat, *chĭ*.	ever changing, *ch'áng-pién*.
wait, *tàng*.	hails, *hiá-pŏ-tsž*.
evening, *wán-sháng*.	snows, *hiá-sŭĭ*.
evening meal, (rice) *wán-*	roars, (sounds) *hiàng*.
fán.	wind, *fūng*.
weather, *t'iēn-k'í (chí)*	past, *kwó-liaù*.
how, what kind, *tsàng-mó-*	rainbow, *t'iēn-hūng*.
yáng.	dew falling, *hiá-lu*.
let us, put *pá* after the	thunders, *tà-lŭi*.
verb.	lighten, *tá-shén*,

go home, *hwüi-kiā.*

there is, *yiù.*

nearly, *cha-pŭ-tō.*

summer, *hía t'iĕn.*

spring, *ch'ặn-t'iĕn.*

winter, *lŭng-t'iĕn.*

autumn, *tsiú-t'iĕn.*

very, *tsüi,* (superlative)

cold, *làng.*

dark, *yĭn.*

damp, *ch'aŭ k'i (chi)*

cannot see, *k'án-pŭ-kiĕn.*

a gale, storm, *paú-fūng.*

to rain, *hiá-yù.*

hard, (of raining) *haù.*

blow, *chuī.*

high, *kaū* or *tá.*

sign, proof, *p'íng-k'ŭ (chü.)*

fall, *hiá,* or *lŏ.*

late, (of evening) *wán.*

go, *k'ŭ (chü)*

still there is, *hwán-yiù.*

forenoon, *sháng-wù.*

one o'clock, *yĭ-hiú-chŭng.*

time, *shí-heú.*

hot, *jĭ.*

like, *swàn.*

trees, *shiú-mŭ.*

budded, *fă-yă.*

pá is a permissive particle, final.

The day is very fine. The sun is going to set. Wait a while, it will soon be dark. If you walk fast, you will be wearied. Eat your evening meal. How is the weather? The weather is cold. The sky is overcast. This evening it is fine weather. It is damp. It is cloudy; I cannot see the stars. It is a gale. The weather is ever changing. It rains hard. It hails, It snows. It thunders. The thunder roars. It lightens. The wind blows. The wind is high. The storm is past, we can see the rainbow. It is a sign of fair weather. The dew is falling. It is not late. Let us go home! There is time (enough) yet, it is still forenoon. It is nearly one o'clock. Do you like this season? Spring is the best. This weather is pleasant; it is neither hot nor cold. This is not like spring; it is like winter. The trees have not yet budded. This summer is very hot.

VOCABULARY.

A, (one),	*yĭ* and *yĭ-kó.*
Abacus,	*swán-p'án.*
Ability,	*t'sâi-nặng, pàn-sź.*
Abolish,	*c'hŭ.*
About,	*c'hā-pŭ-tō.*
Above,	*sháng, tsaí-sháng.*
Accept,	*sheŭ-nŭ.*
Accuse falsely,	*sō-tsúng.*
Acknowledge (to),	*c'híng-jín.*
Across,	*háng-tī.*
Add, (to)	*tiēn-sháng, kiā (chiā .*
Affect,	*kàn-túng.*
After three days,	*heŭ-sān t'iēn.*
Afternoon, (in the)	*hiá-wū.*
Afterwards,	*heŭ-lâi.*
After,	*heŭ-lâi, kĕ, ĭ-héu.*
Agar Agar.	*haĭ-t'saí.*
Again,	*tsaí.*
Age, (old)	*c'háng-sheú.*
Agree (not),	*pŭ-tüí.*

Air, to,	*liang.*
Also,	*yè.*
All,	*tū, tsŭen.*
All round,	*sź-mién.*
Almonds,	*híng-jín.*
Already,	*ì-kīng.*
Altogether,	*kúng-tsùng.*
Alum,	*pă-fân.*
Alum (green),	*ts'īng-fân.*
Ambush,	*maî-fŭ.*
American drills,	*síe-wằn pú.*
Among them,	*nüí-chūng.*
Amount,	*kí-chúng.*
Amputate,	*lâ-hiá.*
Ancestor of 4th degree,	*kaū-tsù.*
Ancestral temple,	*sź-t'âng.*
Ancestors,	*tsù-tsūng.*
Angry (to be),	*túng-ch'í (k'í).*
Apply the mind,	*liŭ-sīn.*
Anchor,	*mâu.*
Announce,	*t'ūng-paú.*
Another, again,	*yiú.*
Another day,	*kài-jĭ.*
Ancient men,	*kù-jín.*
And,	*hô, hwân-haî.*

Animals wild,	*yè-sheú.*
Aniseed (oil),	*pă-kiaù yiû.*
Aniseed (star),	*pă-kiaù.*
Aniseed (broken),	*pă-kiaù chā.*
Ant,	*mâ-ĭ.*
Arm,	*pí, sheù-pí.*
Arrest,	*kû.*
Arch,	*hwân.*
Arch (memorial),	*p'âi-leû.*
Arts, (military)	*wù-í.*
Arts, (ingenious)	*kí-í.*
Arsenic,	*sín-shĭ.*
Assist,	*sīang-pāng.*
Assistant,	*hò-kí.*
Ass,	*lû-tsź.*
Asafœtida,	*ngō-weí.*
Ascend,	*sháng.*
At home, (not)	*pŭ-tsai.*
At home,	*tsaí-kiā (chīa).*
At last,	*mŭ-heú.*
Axletree,	*c'hĕ-chêŭ*
At once,	*tsĭ-k'ĕ̆.*
At, to be at, or in,	*tsaí.*
At present,	*hién-tsai, and jŭ-kīn.*
Autumn,	*t'sīu.*

Average,	*pŭ-tá pŭ-siaú.*
Avoid,	*mién.*
Axe,	*fù-tsż.*

B.

Bad,	*pŭ-haù.*
Baggage trunk,	*híng-sīang.*
Bamboo,	*chŭ.*
Bamboo grove,	*chŭ-lîn.*
Bamboo ware,	*chŭ-c'hí (kí).*
Bamboo poles,	*chŭ-kān.*
Bangles,	*liaú-sheù chŭ.*
Baptize,	*shī-sż.*
Bare the shoulder (to),	*t'ān-hiá.*
Basin stand,	*p'ên-chiá (kia).*
Battery,	*p'aú-t'aî.*
Bathe,	*sż-tsaù.*
Beat (to),	*tà.*
Beat to death,	*tà-sź.*
Beat clothes,	*shwaī.*
Beaver skin,	*haż-ló p'í.*
Bean oil,	*teù.*
Beat gongs,	*tà-lô.*
Beat drums,	*tà-kù.*

Bamboo divining rods,	*t'sīen.*
Because,	*yin-weí,*
Bee hive,	*mĭ-fung wō.*
Bees'-wax,	*pă-lă.*
Bedstead, or bed.	*c'hwáng.*
Be diligent,	*yúng-kŭng.*
Before,	*tāng.*
Before, (coram)	*míen-t'síen.*
Before (ante),	*sĭēn, sĭēn-shí.*
Begin (to),	*k'ĭ, (chĭ).*
Begin work,	*túng-kŭng.*
Beg favour,	*t'aŭ-kwāng.*
Beg,	*yaú, k'iŭ, kĭ.*
Behind,	*hcŭ-mién.*
Be in office,	*tsó-kwān.*
Believe,	*sīang-sín*
Below,	*hia, tsaí-hiú.*
Bend,	*wān.*
Benefit,	*yĭ-c'hú, lĭ-yĭ.*
Besiege,	*weí-k'iuén.*
Be saved,	*tĕ-kiú.*
Betel-nut cake.	*pīng-lăng kaù.*
Betel-nut	*pīng-lăng.*
Beyond the border,	*pīen-waí.*
Birmah,	*Mīen-tíen.*

Birds'-nest,	_yén-hú._
Bind,	_k'wùn-pàng._
Black,	_hě._
Blue lime,	_t'sīng-hweī._
Blankets,	_c'hwâng-chān._
Bleached,	_p'iaū-pě._
Blind,	_hiǎ._
Blood-vessel,	_hǔ-kwàn._
Blow, (to)	_kwǎ._
Body,	_shīn-t'í._
Boil (to),	_chū._
Bolt (to),	_shàn._
Bombazettes,	_yǔ-c'heú._
Book,	_shū, pặn-shū._
Book-style,	_wặn-lì._
Book of filial piety,	_Hiaú-kīng._
Bookcase.	_shū-chiá (kia)._
Book box.	_shū-sīang._
Bookworm,	_tū-ú._
Boots,	_hiüě._
Border custom-house,	_kwān-k'eú._
Born,	_sāng-c'hǔ-!aí._
Born into the world,	_c'hǔ-shí._
Bottle,	_p'íng._

Brass wire,	*hwǎng-t'úng sē.*
Brass foil,	*t'úng-pŏ.*
Brass ware,	*hwǎng-t'úng c'hí (k'i).*
Brass buttons,	*hwǎng-t'úng niù-k'eú.*
Brass nails,	*hwǎng-t'úng tīng.*
Bread,	*mǎn-t'éú.*
Bream,	*chī-û.*
Break in pieces	*c'hiaū-sùi.*
Bricks,	*chuĕn.*
Brick couch,	*k'áng.*
Bridge,	*k'iaû.*
Bring (to),	*nǎ-laî, tsǔ-lai.*
Broad,	*k'wān-tsè.*
Broadcloth,	*tō-lò-nì.*
Broken,	*p'ó.*
Brush (to),	*shwǎ.*
Buddha,	*Fǔ.*
Buddhist deities, (2d class)	*p'ǔ-sǎ.*
Buddhist deities, (3d class)	*lò-hán.*
Buddhist monasteries,	*shí-yúén.*
Buddhist priest,	*hó-sháng.*
Buddhist religion,	*Fǔ-kíau.*
Buffalo horns,	*meú-chiaù (kiŏ)*
Bug,	*c'heú-c'hûng.*

Build (to),	*kaí.*
Build a house,	*kién-ŭ.*
Bunting,	*yù-pú.*
Bury,	*tsáng-maí.*
Burn (to),	*c'haù-hû.*
Burn (to),	*c'hiū.*
Burnt tiles,	*wà.*
Burn incense,	*shaū-hīang.*
Burn paper.	*shaū-chí.*
But,	*tán-shí.*
Butter,	*niû-yiû.*
Butterfly,	*hu-t'iĕ.*
Button,	*niù.*
Button-hole,	*niù-k'eù.*
Buy (to),	*maì.*
By,	*yiû, yúng.*

C.

Calculate,	*swán-cháng.*
Calculate,	*swán, swán-kí.*
Call,	*kiaú.*
Call,	*chaū (kiaú) hú.*
Call out,	*jāng.*
Camagon,	*maû shí.*

Camel,	*lŏ-t'ô.*
Camel's hair,	*lŏ-t'ô maŭ.*
Camlets (Dutch),	*Hŏ-lân yŭ-twán.*
Camlets, (English)	*Yíng-kwŏ yŭ-shā.*
Camlets,	*ŭ-maŭ.*
Camphor,	*chăng-naù.*
Can,	*năng, k'ŏ-ĭ.*
Can,	*năng-keŭ.*
Can walk,	*hwei-tseù.*
Canals and rivers,	*shuì-lú.*
Candareen,	*fặn.*
Cantharides,	*ᶨān-maŭ.*
Cap,	*maŭ-tsᵌ.*
Capital,	*pặn-t'síen.*
Capoor cutchery,	*sān-naí.*
Caraway,	*yuên-suī.*
Carefully reckon,	*sí-swán.*
Carriage,	*c'hē-tsᵌ.*
Carp,	*li-ŭ.*
Carry,	*tai, nă-laí.*
Carry a letter,	*tai-sín.*
Carry (to),	*tài.*
Carry loads,	*t'iaū-tàn.*
Carry (with a yoke),	*t'iaū.*
Carry (of two persons),	*t'ai.*

Carry water,	*t'iaū-shuì.*
Carry on back,	*t'ô.*
Cassia oil,	*k'weí-p'í yeû.*
Cast,	*p'aū.*
Cash,	*t'síen, tûng-t'sièn.*
Cask,	*t'àng.*
Cassia lignea,	*kweí-p'í.*
Cassia buds,	*kweí-tsż.*
Cassia twigs,	*kwei-chi.*
Cassimeres,	*siaù-ní.*
Cat,	*mâu.*
Catty,	*kīn.*
Catch,	*tà-k'ín.*
Cause,	*kiaú*
Cease,	*t'ang.*
Centipede,	*wû-kūng.*
Chair,	*ì, or ì-tsż.*
Chair,	*ì-tsż.*
Chalk mark,	*hweī-yín.*
Change,	*yĭ-cháng.*
Chant prayers,	*níen-kīng.*
Characters,	*tsż.*
Cheap,	*tsíen.*
Certainly,	*pĭ-tíng.*
Chest,	*hiung-t'âng.*

Cheat (to),	*p'ién.*
Chief boatman,	*c'huén-chù.*
China,	*Chŭng-kwŏ.*
China root,	*t'ù-fŭ ling.*
China Proper,	*Nŭi-ti.*
Chinese jam,	*shān-yau.*
Chinese coal,	*t'ù-mei.*
Chinese mile,	*lĭ.*
Chintz,	*hwà-yáng pú.*
Chief minister,	*tsai-siáng.*
Choose,	*chien-slüen.*
Cinnabar,	*chŭ-shā.*
Cinnamon,	*jŭ-kwei.*
Clean,	*kān-tsíng.*
Cleanse to,	*sīng t'sīng.*
Clear (to the mind),	*míng-pĕ.*
Clear (to the eye),	*t'sīng-shwàng.*
Clothes,	*ī-fŭ.*
Cloves,	*tīng·hīang.*
Clever,	*líng-lŭng, líng-lí.*
Clocks,	*tsź-míng-chŭng.*
Cluster of houses,	*chwang.*
Coat of mail,	*chiă (kiă).*
Cocoons,	*t'sǎn-chien.*
Cochin China,	*Ngān-nǎn.*

Coffin and case,	*kwǎn-kwŏ.*
Cold,	*hǎn.*
Cold,	*lang.*
Cold,	*liang.*
Collar,	*lìng-tsż.*
Colour,	*yên-sĕ.*
Column of characters,	*t'áng.*
Come (to),	*lai.*
Come directly,	*tsiú-lai.*
Commentary,	*chú-kìai.*
Common,	*siûn-c'hāng.*
Common seal,	*t'û shū.*
Comply (to),	*ī-t'súng.*
Conduct (to),	*p'ìn-híng.*
Confer royal title,	*fūng.*
Condemn (to),	*tíng-tsüí.*
Confess (to),	*jín-tsüí.*
Congratulate (to),	*kùng-hì.*
Connect (to),	*tsiĕ-sǔ. liĕn.*
Conquer (to),	*tĕ-shíng.*
Cough (to),	*kĕ-seú.*
Conscience,	*liang-sīn.*
Connected,	*sīang-líen.*
Consider about,	*shāng-liǎng.*
Constant,	*c'hǎng.*

Cook (to),	*tsó-fán, shaú.*
Cooking range,	*tsaú-t'eú.*
Cool,	*fūng-liang.*
Copper ore,	*sāng t'úng.*
Cornelians,	*mâ-naù.*
Cornelian beads,	*mâ-naù chū.*
Coral,	*sān-hú.*
Corpse,	*sž-shī.*
Cotton cloth,	*pú.*
Cotton,	*míen-hwā.*
Cotton thread,	*míen-síen.*
Cotton-seed oil,	*míen-hwa yiú.*
Counter,	*kwei.*
Court,	*c'haú-t'íng.*
Cover over,	*kai-haù.*
Cover (to),	*kai-sháng.*
Covet (to),	*t'ān.*
Cow,	*meû.*
Cows' milk,	*meû-naȝ.*
Crane,	*síen-hau.*
Crape,	*hú-cheū.*
Crack,	*liĕ-k'aī.*
Cricket,	*c'hǔ-c'hû.*
Crisp,	*t'suí.*
Crooked,	*siê.*

Crossbow arrow,	*nù-tsíen*
Cross beams,	*hûng-liang.*
Crush (to),	*yă-hwaí.*
Cry,	*chiaú, (kiaú).*
Cubebs,	*c'híng-c'hiĕ.*
Cucumber,	*wâng-kwā.*
Cultivated land,	*t'iên-tí.*
Cupboard,	*kweí.*
Cure (to),	*chí-haù.*
Curiosities,	*kù-náu.*
Cup,	*peī.*
Curtain,	*cháng-tsż.*
Custom-house,	*haì-kwān.*
Cutch,	*û-c'hâ.*
Cut,	*lâ.*
Cut (with knife),	*kŏ.*
Cut (with scissors),	*tsìen.*
Cut off the hand,	*chàn-sheù.*
Cut open,	*kŏ-h'aī.*

D.

Damask,	*twán-pú.*
Damask silk,	*hwā-twán, líng.*
Damp,	*c'haû.*

Dangerous,	*lì-haí.*
Dark,	*ngán.*
Dates (black),	*hě-tsaù.*
Dates (red),	*húng-tsaù.*
Daughter (your),	*líng-ngaí.*
Day,	*t'iēn, jǐ.*
Day's work,	*yǐ-kūng.*
Day after to-morrow,	*heú-t'iēn.*
Day before yesterday,	*t'síen-jǐ.*
Dear (opp. cheap),	*kweí,* (opp. *tsiên*).
Death (freeze to),	*túng-sź.*
Decide (to),	*tíng-kweī.*
Deck planks,	*t'sāng-pàn.*
Deed of sale,	*wận-yŏ.*
Deep, `	*shīn-t'sèen.*
Deer horns,	*lú-chiàu,* (*kiŏ*).
Deer and buffalo horns,	*lǔ-níu chīn.*
Defeat (to),	*paí-cháng.*
Defeated,	*shū.*
Delay (to),	*tān-kŏ.*
Deliberate (to),	*chīn-chŏ, shāng-liầng.*
Deliver down (to),	*c'hûen-hiá.*
Depend on (to),	*í-laí.*
Descend, (to)	*chíang-hía laí.*
Desire (to),	*yuén.*

Desist (to),	*chí-chú.*
Despair (to),	*tsü-wáng.*
Destroy (to),	*hweí-hwaî.*
Detain (to),	*líu-chŏ.*
Die (to),	*c'hŭ-shí, sz.*
Differ (to),	*c'hā-chŏ.*
Different,	*làang-yáng.*
Difficult (to do),	*nân-tsó-tĭ.*
Dig open,	*kiŭ-k'āi.*
Dig (to),	*kiŭ.*
Diligent (be),	*yúng-kūng.*
Dimities,	*líen-t'íau pú.*
Diminish,	*chìen-shàu.*
Dining-table,	*fán-chŏ.*
Dinner spread,	*paì-fán.*
Dinner (take),	*c'hĭ-fán.*
Direct (to),	*chi·tìen.*
Disclose (to),	*lŭ-c'hŭ-laî.*
Discord (sow),	*t'ìau-sō.*
Discuss (to),	*píen-lún.*
Dish,	*p'ên-tsž.*
Disperse (to),	*sán-k'áī.*
Disregard (to),	*pŭ-kú.*
Dissolve (to),	*siaū-hwá.*
Distinguish (to),	*fặn-míng.*

Distinct,	*t'sĭng-c'hŭ.*
District,	*híen.*
Disturb,	*chìau-túng.*
Divide (to),	*fận-k'aĭ.*
Divine,	*chău-pŭ.*
Divine (to),	*k'íu-t'ien.*
Do (to),	*tsó, tsŏ-weí.*
Doe skin,	*c'hí-p'í.*
Dog,	*keù, kiuén.*
Dollar,	*yǎng-tsiận.*
Dollar (Mexican),	*yīng-yǎng.*
Dollar (one tenth of),	*kiŏ.*
Domestics, (trade term)	*hwǎ-c'hí pú.*
Done,	*haù.*
Door,	*mận-t'eŭ.*
Door-front,	*t'siận-mận.*
Dove,	*kŏ-tsz̀.*
Dragon's-blood gum,	*hiŭ-chíèh.*
Drake,	*yè-yă.*
Draw,	*lā.*
Draw to (pictures),	*hwá.*
Dried prawns,	*hĭa-mì.*
Dried mussels,	*tán-t'saí.*
Drink wine,	*hŏ-tsìu.*
Drink again.	*tsai-hŏ.*

Drink together,	*tüí-yìn.*
Drive (to),	*kàn.*
Drums (to beat),	*tà-kù.*
Dry,	*kān.*
Dry in the sun,	*shaí, shaí-kān.*
Duck,	*yă-tsż.*
Duck eggs,	*yă-tán.*
Duck (mandarin),	*yuēn-yāng.*
Duck-keeper,	*k'ān-yă tž jín.*
Dutch camlets,	*Hô-lán yù-twán.*
Duty,	*pàn-fạn.*
Duties (public),	*kūng-shí.*
Dwell,	*chú, kú, chū-chú.*
Dye, green,	*lú-chīau.*
Dye, indigo,	*t'ú-tíen.*

E

Each, every,	*kŏ,*
Earth,	*tí.*
Early,	*tsaù.*
Earth-worm,	*c'hŭ-c'hŭ.*
Earth bricks (large),	*p'ī.*
Easy,	*yûng-í.*
Eastward,	*híang-tūng.*

East of the Drum tower, *Kù-leû tūng.*

Eat (to), *ch'ĭ (k'ĭ).*

Eat enough, *ch'ĭ-paù.*

Eat meat, *ch'ĭ-jŭ.*

Eat habitually, *ch'ĭ-kwān.*

Eat books, *ch'ĭ-shū.*

Ebony, *wū-mŭ.*

Economical, *shàng-kién.*

Eel (white), *pĕ-shén.*

Eel (yellow), *hwáng-shén.*

Eight, *pă.*

Ells long, *pĭ chĭ.*

Emperor, *Hwâng-sháng.*

Empty, *k'ūng.*

Employ men, *shí hwán.*

Endure (to), *jìn naí.*

Engrave, *k'ĕ-tsź.*

Enjoy to (life), *hìang-shęú.*

Enough (not), *pū-tsŭ.*

Enquire (to), *là-t'īng.*

Enter (to), *tsín, tsín-c'hǜ.*

Entice (to), *yìn-yeù.*

Entire, *chèng.*

Enter the ground, *jŭ-t'ù.*

Entrust (to), *t'ŏ-fú.*

Ermine skin,	*yín-shù p'í.*
Escape suffering,	*l'ŏ nán.*
Escort,	*hú-súng, súng.*
Escort guests,	*súng-kĕ.*
Essays,	*wặn-chăng.*
Establish a capital,	*kíen-tū.*
Everywhere,	*kŏ-c'hú.*
Every year,	*meī-níen.*
Examine (to),	*k'aù-chien.*
Exceedingly (initial),	*hặn.*
Exceedingly (final),	*tĕ-hặn.*
Exchange,	*tuí-hwán.*
Except,	*ì-naí.*
Exert yourself,	*c'hù-líh.*
Exhalations,	*tù-c'hí.*
Explanation,	*kìai shwŏ.*
Expend,	*k'aī-siaū.*
Expand (to),	*shīn-k'wān.*
Extinguish (to),	*miĕ-mú.*
Extraordinary,	*kĕ-waí.*
Eyes,	*yèn-tsīng.*
Eyes (inflamed),	*fāh-yèn.*

F.

Facing,	*mién-tsż.*
Faint,	*huūn-kwó chú.*
Faint (to),	*fă-hwąn.*
Faithful and honest,	*chūng-heú.*
Fall (to),	*tiĕ-hiá, hiá, lŏ-hiá.*
Fall (to let),	*hiá.*
Fall into snares,	*sháng-táng*
Fall into misfortune,	*tseù-nán.*
False,	*kià.*
Falsely accuse,	*sō-tsúng.*
False coral,	*chìa-sān hû.*
False pearls,	*chìa-chēn chū.*
Famed surgeon,	*mîng-ĭ.*
Family (master of),	*kiā-chū.*
Family name,	*síng.*
Fan (to),	*tà-shén.*
Fans (paper),	*chi-shén.*
Fancy cottons,	*hwā-pú.*
Farther back,	*tsai-sháng.*
Father,	*laù-tsz.*
Favour (beg),	*t'aū-kwāng.*
Favourable,	*shąn.*
Fear (to),	*p'á.*

Fear (pain),	*p'á-túng.*
Fear not,	*pŭ-p'á.*
Feather fans,	*yù-shén.*
Feeble,	*jwàn-jŏ.*
Feed (to),	*weí, yáng.*
Feed pigs,	*weí-chū.*
Feign,	*chià-tsó.*
Felt cuttings,	*chān-suí.*
Felt caps,	*chān-maú.*
Ferry over, (to)	*paì-tú.*
Feet (large),	*tá-kiŏ.*
Feverish,	*fă-shaū.*
Few,	*shaù.*
Few,	*yiù-hién.*
Few of, a little of,	*siē.*
Field spider,	*chū-chū.*
Fight to (of individuals),	*tà-chiá (kiá).*
Fight to (of armies),	*tà-cháng.*
Figured coloured cottons,	*yĕ-hwā si-pú.*
File and rank,	*wù-tuí.*
Filial piety (book of),	*Hiaú-kīng.*
Filial son,	*hiaú-tsż.*
Final interrogative, (pa.)	*ní.*
Fine china ware,	*sí-t'sz c'hí (k'i).*
Fine linen,	*sí-mâ pú.*

Finish (to),	*tsó-wân.*
Finished,	*wân-liaù.*
First,	*sĭen.*
First come,	*sĭen-laí.*
First month,	*c'hing-yŭ*
First day of the month,	*c'hū-jĭ.*
First title of nobility,	*kūng.*
Fire fly,	*yûng-hŏ c'hûng.*
Fireworks,	*paú-chŭ.*
Firm,	*kĭč-shĭ.*
Fish, (to)	*yû, tà-yû*
Fish (fresh),	*sĭen-û.*
Fish (salt),	*hĭen-û.*
Fish (salt),	*yû-hĭen.*
Fish maws,	*yû-tú.*
Fish skins,	*yû-p'i.*
Fish hawk,	*û-yīng.*
Fishing-net,	*là-û wàng.*
Fish-hook,	*tiaú-û keū.*
Five,	*wù.*
Fire-stove,	*hŏ lû.*
Fire cannon,	*fáng-p'aú.*
Five *teu* = one.	*hŭ.*
Five feet (land measure),	*pù.*
Five classics (The),	*Wú-kĭng.*

Fix (to),	*tíng-hiá.*
Flatter (to),	*fung-c'híng.*
Flat yellow pumpkin,	*nân-kwā.*
Flea,	*keù-tsaú.*
Flesh and skin,	*jŭ-p'ì.*
Fling (to),	*jàng.*
Flints,	*hó-shĭ.*
Floating-bridge,	*feū-c'hîau.*
Floor,	*ti-pàn.*
Floss from Canton,	*Kwàng-tung jûng.*
Floss from various provs.	*kŏ-shèng jûng.*
Flour,	*mîen-făn.*
Flow (to),	*liŭ.*
Flowers.	*hwā.*
Flowers (paper),	*chi-hwā.*
Flowers (nutmeg),	*teù-k'eu hwā.*
Flowers and grass,	*hwā-t'saù.*
Flower jar,	*hwā-p'ìng.*
Flower pot,	*hwā-p'ên.*
Fly (to),	*feī, fì.*
Foil (brass),	*t'ûng-pŏ.*
Foil (tin),	*sĭ-pŏ.*
Foment, (to)	*chi-ù c'hwāng.*
Foot,	*c'hŏ.*
Footstool,	*chìau-tâ.*

For me,	*t'ĭ-wǒ.*
For the first time,	*c'hū.*
For (on account of),	*wei, yīn-wei.*
For (to give to),	*keì (kĭ).*
Forbid,	*chín-chi.*
Foreign,	*waí-kwŏ.*
Foreign coal,	*waí-kwŏ mei.*
Forenoon,	*sháng-cheú.*
Forget (to),	*wâng, wâng-kí.*
Fork,	*c'hā-tsž.*
Formerly,	*t'sûng-t'sien.*
Foundation,	*ŭ-kī.*
Four,	*sž.*
Four books (The),	*Sž-shū.*
Fowl,	*kī, chī.*
Fowls' eggs (salted),	*hién-chī-tán.*
Fowl broth,	*kī-t'āng.*
Fowl feathers,	*chī-maû.*
Fox,	*hû-lī.*
Fragrant wood,	*hīang-c'haî.*
Friend,	*p'áng-yiù.*
Freeze (to),	*túng-pīng.*
Freeze to death,	*túng-sž.*
From, along,	*t'sûng.*
From a boy,	*t'sûng-siaù.*

Front door,	*t'sien-mặn.*
Full,	*màn,* or *mwan.*
Fulfil (to),	*c'híng-tsiú.*
Fustians,	*hwei-jûng.*

G.

Galangal,	*líang chīang.*
Gambier,	*tá t'sīng.*
Gamboge,	*l'êng hwǎng.*
Gamble,	*tù t'sien.*
Garden (vegetable),	*t'sai-yuên.*
Garlic,	*swán.*
Garment (appos. for),	*kíen.*
Garroo wood,	*c'hên hīang.*
Gather up (to),	*sheū-shě.*
Gauze,	*shā.*
Gentleman (young),	*kūng-tsż.*
Gild a surface,	*t'û kīn.*
Gild figures,	*míau kīn.*
Gild in spots,	*sà kīn.*
Girl,	*sìau-nā-tsż.*
Give away (to),	*l'uī keì.*
Give (to),	*kǐ, pī.*
Give more (to),	*t'īen.*

Ginghams,	*kŏ sĭ maû pú.*
Give,	*súng.*
Glass,	*pō-lí.*
Glass dressing,	*c'hwēn ī chíng.*
Glass ware (native),	*liaú c'hí.*
Glass beads (native),	*liaú chū.*
Glass (looking),	*maú chíng.*
Glass globe for gold fish,	*pō-lí û kāng*
Glue,	*p'í chíau.*
Go,	*c'hú (k'ú).*
Go to the east,	*hiàng-tūng tseù.*
Go (to),	*tseù, k'ù, wàng.*
Go east (to),	*hiang-tūng.*
Go up a hill,	*sháng-shān.*
Go round, (to)	*jaú chō tseù.*
Goat,	*shān-yâng.*
Goats' hair,	*shān yâng maû.*
Goat-sucker,	*tú chūen.*
God,	*Sháng-tí.*
God of war,	*Kwān-fū-tsz̀.*
Gods, (Tauist)	*shín-taú.*
God of the Tauists,	*Yü-tí.*
God of riches,	*T'sai-shín.*
Goddess of mercy,	*Kwān-yín.*
Gold,	*kīn.*

Gold thread (real),	*chīn chīn-sién.*
Gold thread (imitated),	*chīa chīn-sién.*
Gold ware,	*chīn-c'hí (k'í).*
Gold fish,	*chīn-û̂.*
Gone (having),	*taú-kwó.*
Good,	*haù.*
Goods (embroidered),	*sí eú hí.*
Goose,	*ngô.*
Goose (wild),	*lá yén.*
Goose quills,	*ngô-maû̂.*
Government seal,	*sì, or sz.*
Government offices,	*kwān-tsiŏ.*
Grass,	*t'saù, tsìng-tsaù.*
Grandfather,	*tsù-fú.*
Grave (make a),	*tsó-fạn.*
Great,	*tá-tĭ.*
Great grandfather,	*tsung-tsù.*
Green,	*lŭ-sĭ-tĭ.*
Grove (bamboo),	*chŭ-lín.*
Guest,	*k'ĕ-jìn.*
Grain junk,	*yŭn-líang-c'hwên.*
Grass cloth (fine),	*sí hiá-pú.*
Grass cloth (coarse),	*t'sū hiá-pú.*
Grateful (be),	*paú ngạn.*
Grey squirrel,	*hweī-shù.*

I

Grey shirtings,	*pàn-sĕ yàng-pú.*
Grieve,	*yiŭ-mán.*
Ground-nut cake,	*hwă shēng pìng.*
Grouse,	*shă-chī.*
Guard (to),	*pà-sheù.*
Guess,	*t'sāi.*

H.

Hair,	*t'eû-fă,* or *mau.*
Half a day	*pàn-t'īen.*
Half a month,	*pán kó-yŭ.*
Half a cask,	*pán wăn.*
Half-summer robe,	*sìau-kwá.*
Hall,	*t'âng.*
Hams,	*hò-t'uī.*
Hammer,	*lăng-t'eú.*
Han dynasty,	*Hán-c'haŭ.*
Handicraft,	*sheù-í.*
Handkerchiefs,	*sheù-p'ă.*
Hanging jar,	*kwá-p'íng.*
Hanging bucket,	*tiaŭ-t'ùng.*
Hanging mirror,	*kwá-chíng* (*king*).
Hang-lanthorn,	*kwá-tăng.*
Hard,	*yíng.*

Hare-skins,	*t'ú p'ï.*
Harmony,	*hô.*
Harness a cart (to),	*t'aú-c'hë.*
Hat-stand,	*maú-chiá (kiạ).*
Have,	*yiù.*
Have not,	*mŭ-yiù.*
Having gone,	*taŭ-kwó.*
Hawk,	*yīng.*
He,	*t'ạ.*
He then said,	*tsiú shwŏ.*
Heart,	*sīn-châng.*
Hearth-cricket,	*tsaú-wâng-mà.*
Heaven,	*t'ïen.*
Helmet,	*k'weī.*
Help,	*siāng-pạng.*
Hemp,	*mâ.*
Hempen rope,	*mâ-shìng.*
Here,	*ché-lì.*
Hide,	*t'sạng-nì.*
High,	*kaū.*
Hire,	*tsū.*
Hold (to),	*t'sāng.*
Hold in the mouth,	*hiên.*
Homestead,	*tsĕ-tsż.*
Honey,	*fûng-mì.*

Honey-bee,	*mĭ-fūng.*
Honourable,	*kwei.*
Horizontal,	*hặng.*
Hot,	*jĕ.*
How,	*tsèn-mỏ yáng.*
How many ?	*kĭ-kó.*
House,	*fấng-tsz̀.*
Hungry,	*wó* or *ngó.*
Honoured,	*líng.*
Honest,	*laù-shĭ.*
Horse,	*mà.*
Hot weather,	*t'ien-jĕ.*
House-fly,	*t'sāng-yīng.*
How often ?	*kĭ-hwei.*
How many chapters ?	*kĭ-kiúen.*
How dare I ?	*c'hĭ-kàn ?*
Hu-cheu silk,	*Hû sz̀.*
Humble,	*c'hiēn hū.*
Husks of betel-nut,	*pīng-lấng-ĭ.*

I.

I,	*wỏ.*
I do not understand,	*pŭ tùng.*
I do not want,	*pŭ-yaú.*

I will not,	*pŭ k'ạng.*
If,	*t'àng hŏ.*
Imitate,	*hiŏ.*
Imitation (lasting),	*siaù yŭ lîng.*
Important,	*yaú-kìn.*
Imported,	*yŭn-laî-tĭ.*
In, within,	*tsaí, lì.*
In, am, in, was.	*tsaí.*
In, (on account of),	*weí.*
In the fields,	*t'iên-lì.*
In the city,	*c'hîng-lì.*
In the market,	*shi-sháng.*
In the street,	*kiaî-sháng.*
In the mouth,	*tsuì-lì.*
In the country,	*hĭang-lì, tsaí hiáng-hiá.*
Incense sticks, ،	*shî c'hễn wäng.*
Inch,	*t'sún.*
Inclined,	*siê.*
Incurable,	*ī-pŭ-laí.*
Indian ink,	*mě.*
Indian cow bezoar,	*Yín-tú nĭu-hwâng.*
Indigestion,	*siaū-hwá pŭ-túng.*
Inefficacious,	*pŭ-t'īng.*
Inferior Corean ginseng,	*hiá-tềng Kaū-lí shén.*
Inferior Japan ginseng,	*hiá-tềng Jĭ pền shén.*

Inferior pumelo peel,	*hiá-tèng yeù p'í.*
Inferior paper,	*tsż-tèng chi.*
Inferiors,	*nàn-pei.*
Inform, (to),	*kaú-sú.*
Ingenious,	*líng-c'hìau.*
Ingenious arts,	*k'i-i.*
Injure,	*shāng-haí.*
Injuries,	*hai-c'hú.*
Injury by delay,	*tān-wú.*
Inquire,	*tà-t'īng.*
Insert (to),	*c'hwĕn.*
Inside,	*neí (nüi), lì-mién.*
Instruct,	*chiaú-hiǔn.*
Intelligent,	*t'sūng míng.*
Intelligible,	*c'hīng pǎ.*
Intercept,	*tsiĕ-lán.*
Interest,	*li-t'síen.*
Investigate,	*c'há-c'hǎ.*
Invite,	*tsìng.*
Iron (to),	*t'áng.*
Iron wire,	*tiĕ sī.*
Iron ladle,	*t'sàn-tsż.*
Is, am, &c.	*shí.*
Is called,	*kiaú.*
Is there any ?	*yiù-nī ?*

Is it not so?	*k'ò pŭ shi?*
Isinglass,	*yû-chīau.*
It certainly is not,	*píng pŭ-shi.*
It does not agree,	*pŭ-tuí.*
It does not concern,	*pŭ-kwān.*
It differs little,	*c'hā-pŭ-tò.*
It is so,	*chō.*
It is not wrong,	*pŭ-tsó.*
It is not so,	*pŭ-shi.*
It is not far from it.	*pŭ-lî.*
It is very different,	*c'hā-yuèn.*
It is very true,	*hặn-shí.*
It is just,	*tsiú-shí.*
It is then correct,	*t'saî-shi.*
It is as before,	*yuén-shí.*
It is not certain,	*pŭ-chùn.*
It is pretty,	*yiù-t'sù.*
It is not pretty,	*mū-t'sù.*
It matters not which,	*piĕ-chū.*
It must be,	*tsùng-shí.*
It will do,	*k'ò-ì.*
It will not do,	*pŭ lîng.*
Ivory ware,	*siáng-yâ c'hí.*

J.

Jar,	*p'íng-tsž.*
Jacket,	*mà-kwá.*
Japan wax,	*Ji-pàn lă.*
Japanese ginseng (best),	*sháng têng Jĭ pèn shén.*
Japanese ginseng (inf.),	*hiá-têng Jĭ-pèn shén.*
Jaundice,	*hwâng-chéng.*
Jesus,	*Yê-sū.*
Jetty,	*mã-t'eû.*
Join battle,	*kiaŭ-fúng.*
Judge (to),	*shĕn-shi.*
Jump,	*t'iaŭ.*
Just come,	*t'sai-lai.*
Just,	*kŭng-p'íng.*
Just as,	*chíng-tsaî.*
Just now,	*t'sai-kăng.*

K.

Keep (to),	*sheŭ.*
Keep watch,	*k'àn-kīng.*
Kettle,	*shuž-hû.*
King,	*wâng.*
Kingfisher feathers,	*t'sui-maŭ.*

Kitchen,	*c'hŭ-fâng.*
Kitchen cupboard,	*c'hŭ-kwei.*
Kneading-board,	*mien-pàn.*
Kneel,	*t'sìng.*
Kneel and bow,	*kwei-pai.*
Knife,	*taŭ.*
Knot, (tie a)	*kwei.*
Know (to),	*hiaù-tè.*
Kranjee wood,	*Yă-lân-chĭ mŭ.*

L.

Lacquered ware,	*c'hī-c'hí.*
Lakka wood,	*chiáng-hīang.*
Lamp,	*tặng.*
Lamp-wicks,	*tặng-t'saù.*
Lan, a kind of silk,	*lô.*
Land cultivated,	*t'iên-tí.*
Land (owner of),	*tí-chù.*
Land otter-skin,	*t'ă-p'í.*
Language,	*hwá.*
Large cash,	*tá-t'siên.*
Large house, or office,	*c'hàng.*
Large fox-skins,	*tá hŭ-lu p'í.*
Large bason,	*tá-p'ên.*

Large earthen water-vessel.	*kăng.*
Large earth bricks,	*p'ĭ.*
Last year,	*c'hŭ-niên.*
Lasting,	*laû.*
Lazy,	*làn-tŭ.*
Lead,	*yìn-taŭ.*
Lead (white),	*c'hīen-fạn.*
Lead (yellow),	*hŭ̆ng-tăn.*
Lead (in pigs),	*c'hīen-k'weí.*
Lead (in sheets),	*c'hīen-p'ién.*
Lead soldiers (to),	*lìng-pīng.*
Leading-mule,	*pīen-t'aŭ.*
Lean (to),	*k'aŭ.*
Leap into a river,	*t'eû-hí.*
Leap into a well,	*t'eû-tsing.*
Learn (to),	*hiŏ.*
Leather trunks,	*p'í-sīang.*
Leather boxes, for holding silver,	*p'í-kăng.*
Leather articles,	*p'í-c'hí (k'í).*
Leave it there,	*liû-chŏ.*
Leave a place,	*lí-k'aī.*
Leggings,	*t'aŭ-k'ŭ.*
Lend,	*tsié.*

Leopard-skins,	*paú-p'í.*
Lest,	*k'ùng-p'á.*
Let,	*c'hŭ-jín.*
Let fall (to),	*hiá.*
Let fall hair,	*tiaú-maú.*
Letter-boat,	*sín-c'hwên.*
Letter-office,	*sín-kŭ.*
Letters (appositive for),	*fūng.*
Lettuce,	*shąng-t'saí.*
Library,	*shū-fång.*
Lichee,	*lí-chí.*
Lie down,	*miên-hiá.*
Lie down,	*t'āng.*
Lie (falsely),	*hwàng-hwá.*
Lies,	*hwāng-t'áng.*
Life, (soul)	*síng míng.*
Life (the whole),	*chūng-shīn.*
Lift,	*chŭ-c'hì.*
Light, (opp. to heavy)	*c'hīng.*
Light, (opp. to darkness)	*liång-kwāng.*
Light books,	*hiên-shū.*
Light the stove,	*shąng hwò-lú.*
Lime,	*pă-hweī.*
Lime,	*shŭ-hweī.*
Lime (blue),	*t'sīng-hweī.*

Lining,	*lì-tsź.*
Liquid indigo,	*shiù-tián.*
Liquorice,	*kān-t'saù.*
Literary name,	*haú.*
Little,	*siaù.*
Little (a) (time &c.)	*yĭ-hwci.*
Little boy,	*siaù-hai-tsź.*
Live again,	*fŭ-hwŏ.*
Local banditti,	*t'ù-feì (fì).*
Long, length,	*c'háng-twàn.*
Long since,	*laù-tsaù.*
Long time,	*c'háng-kiù.*
Long ells,	*pĭ-chì.*
Long robe,	*c'háng-shān.*
Long robe with waistband.	*p'aû-tsź.*
Long summer robe,	*tá-kwá.*
Long stool,	*pàn-tēng.*
Long high table,	*t'iaû-ngán.*
Look,	*k'án.*
Look (after),	*chaú-yīng.*
Loose light.	*sūng.*
Lose (to),	*pŭ-kién.*
Lose capital,	*shĭ-pạn.*
Lotus,	*ngeù.*
Lotus roots,	*hô-hwā.*

Lotus nets,   *líen-tsz̀.*

Low,   *tī.*

Louse,   *sz̄-tsz̀.*

Lucralan seed,   *tá-fēng-tsz̀.*

Lung ngan, (a fruit)   *kweí-yuên.*

Lute-string,   *chiuén.*

Lying in the W.   *k'aú-sī.*

M.

Mace, one-tenth of an oz. *t'siên.*

Mackerel,   *tz̀-û̂.*

Made to order,   *tíng-tsó-tĭ.*

Magistrate,   *chi-híen.*

Magpie,   *hz̀-c'hiŭ.*

Make (to),   *tsó.*

Make a prostration,   *k'ŭ-t'eû.*

Make a hedge,   *lí-pā.*

Make a grave,   *tsó-fạ̈n.*

Make up a deficit,   *pù-tsŭ.*

Make up money (to),   *ch'au.*

Man,   *jín.*

Man (old),   *laù jín-kiā (chia).*

Manage,   *kwàn-lz̀.*

Manchunan ginseng,   *kwān-tūng jẹ̈n-shên.*

Mandarin's seal,	*yín,*
Mandarin duck,	*yuĕn-yāng.*
Mandarin's office,	*yâ-mặn.*
Mangrove bark,	*k'aù-p'í.*
Manila cordage,	*Lû-sūng shîng.*
Manufactured copper,	*shēn-t'ûng.*
Manufactured iron,	*shēn-t'iĕ.*
Manure cakes,	*k'ēng-shâ.*
Many,	*tŏ.*
Marble slabs,	*yûn-shĭ.*
Mark,	*tà-yín.*
Martin,	*yén-tsż.*
Martin skin,	*tīau-p'í.*
Mason,	*ni-nà-tsíang.*
Master,	*tūng-kīa (chia).*
Master of a family,	*kīa-chū.*
Mast,	*c'huên-weî.*
Mast lanthorn,	*weî-tặng.*
Masts & spars (hard wood),	*chúng-mŭ-wei.*
Masts & spars (soft wood),	*c'hīng-mŭ-weî.*
Match,	*p'eí-chĭ.*
Matter (a),	*sż-t'síng,* or *sż-t'ż.*
May,	*k'ŏ-ż.*
Mean (my),	*hān-pi.*
Measure (to),	*líang.*

Measures and weights,	*teù-c'héng.*
Measure of five feet,	*pú-kūng.*
Meet,	*ú-chō.*
Meet (to),	*páng-kién.*
Member of a Board,	*lâng-chūng.*
Memorial arch,	*p'aî-leû.*
Men (appositive for),	*kó.*
Mend,	*siù.*
Merit,	*kūng-tĕ.*
Messenger,	*c'haî-sháng.*
Messenger's room,	*pān-fâng.*
Method,	*fă-tsż.*
Meu and a half,	*meù-pán.*
Middle man,	*chūng-jîn.*
Migratory locust,	*hwâng-c'hûng.*
Mile (English),	*sān-lì.*
Mile (Chinese),	*lì.*
Mind, (heart)	*sīn.*
Mirror-stand,	*chíng-t'aī (king).*
Misery,	*k'ù.*
Mix,	*t'iaû hô.*
Mock,	*hí-lúng.*
Moist,	*shi.*
Mole cricket,	*t'ù-keù.*
Molest,	*nân-weî.*

Money,	*t'siên, tûng-t'siên.*
Money return (to),	*hwàn.*
Month (a),	*yŭ.*
Month (first),	*chíng-yŭ.*
Moon (the),	*yŭ-líang.*
Mortar,	*ní.*
Mother cloves,	*mù-tīng-hīang.*
Mosquito,	*wận-tsż.*
Mosquito net,	*wận-cháng.*
Most, (sign of super.)	*tìng.*
Mother,	*níang.*
Mother-of-pearl shell,	*yûn-mù-c'hiau.*
Mother-of-pearl ware,	*yûn-mù c'hiaú-c'hí.*
Mule,	*ló-tsż.*
Musical box,	*pă-yīn c'hín.*
Musk,	*shŏ-hīang.*
Muslin,	*yáng-shā.*
Must not,	*pŭ-tĕ.*
Mutually,	*sīang-ừ.*
My cottage,	*shé-hiá.*
My vill　e,	*pận-hīang.*
Myrrh,	*mŏ-yŏ.*

N.

Nail, (a),	*tīng.*
Nail (to),	*tíng.*
Name,	*míng-tsź,c'hì-míng.*
Name (proper),	*míng.*
Name (literary),	*haú.*
Name (to),	*c'hīng.*
Narrow,	*chă.*
Native glass ware,	*liaú-c'hí.*
Native glass beads,	*liaú-chū.*
Near,	*sīang-kín.*
Near road,	*kín-lú.*
Needle,	*chīn.*
Needle-guard,	*tì-chīn.*
Neighbours,	*lín-shé.*
New,	*sīn.*
News,	*sín-sǐ, sín·wán.*
Next year,	*laí-nîen.*
Night (at), evening,	*wán-sháng.*
Nine,	*kiù.*
Nod the head to,	*tìen-t'eû.*
North of the temple,	*kūng-peì (pě).*
Northern mountains,	*pě-shān.*
Northwards,	*pě-mién.*

K

Not,	*pŭ.*
Not much,	*yiù-hién* (limit).
Not fear,	*pŭ-p'á.*
Not to care for,	*pŭ-lì.*
Not at home,	*pŭ-tsai.*
Not the same,	*pŭ-t'ûng.*
Not dare,	*pŭ-kàn.*
Not enough,	*pŭ-tsŭ.*
Not to acknowledge,	*pŭ c'hīng-jín.*
Not only,	*pŭ-chì.*
Not willing,	*pŭ-k'àng.*
Not well,	*pŭ-shū-fŭ.*
Not in good spirits,	*pŭ-shwàng-k'wai.*
Noted surgeon,	*hwá-tó.*
Novels,	*slau-shwŏ.*
Now,	*kīn.*
Nutmeg flowers,	*teù-k'eú hwā.*
Nutmegs,	*jŭ-k'eú hwā.*
Nut galls,	*wŭ-pei-tsż.*

O.

Oar,	*tsiáng.*
Obey,	*tsūn-t'súng.*
Obliquely,	*kwai-wān-ạr.*

Obtain fame (to),	c'hŭ-míng.
Occasionally,	ngeǔ-ǫr.
Offend,	kān-fán.
Office servants, (at mines)	c'hàng-tīng.
Oil,	yiû.
Oil of gum benjamin,	ngān-sǐ yiû.
Oil of the dyandra tree,	t'ûng-yiû.
Oil of palma christi,	pí-mâ yiû.
Oil paintings,	yiû-t'sǐ hwá.
Oiled paper,	yiû-chi.
Old,	c'hiú (kiú).
Old deer horns,	laù-lǔ jûng.
Olibanum, (frankincense)	jû-hīang.
On the South,	nǎn-pīen.
On the street,	kiaī-shǎng.
On the bridge,	c'hiaû-shǎng.
On this side,	ché-pīen.
On that side,	ná-pīen.
Once,	yǐ-t'sź.
One,	yǐ.
One week,	yǐ-kí lǐ-paí.
One kind,	yǐ-híang.
One day's work,	yǐ-kūng.
One parcel,	yǐ-paū.
One meu,	yǐ-meù.

Onions,	*t'sŭng, t'sŭng-t'eŭ.*
Only,	*pŭ-kwó.*
Open a shop,	*k'aï-tién.*
Open a book,	*k'aï-kiuén.*
Opium,	*Ya-pien, yǎng-yŏ.*
Oppose,	*chŭ-chŭ.*
Opposite,	*tui-kwó.*
Orange-peel,	*c'hén-p'i.*
Orderly,	*t'si-chĭng.*
Orderly conduct (custom),	*kweï-kù.*
Ordinary meal,	*pién-fán.*
Other,	*piě.*
Ought,	*yĭng-tăng; yĭng-kaï.*
Ought not,	*pŭ-p'ei.*
Outside,	*waï-t'eŭ.*
Ounce,	*yĭ-liàng.*
Outside the city,	*c'hĭng-waï.*
Overturn,	*t'uï-taū.*
Owner of land,	*ti-chù.*
Oyster shells,	*lĭ-c'hiaú.*

P.

Pacify people,	*ngān-mín*
Pain,	*t'ūng.*
Paint,	*yiû-c'hĭ.*
Paint (to),	*sháng-c'hĭ.*
Pair (a),	*shwāng.*
Palsy,	*t'ān-fūng.*
Palpitation of the heart,	*sĭn-t'iaú.*
Palampore,	*míen-pei t'aī.*
Paper,	*chi.*
Parch (to),	*kān-t'iĕ.*
Parrot,	*yíng-kō.*
Parsley,	*c'hĭn-t'sai.*
Pass,	*kwó.*
Pass the night,	*sŭ.*
Paste up (to),	*t'iĕ-c'hŭ.*
Pattern,	*yáng-tsž.*
Pay custom,	*wân-shuí.*
Peacock,	*k'ùng-c'hiŏ.*
Peacock feathers,	*k'ùng-t'siŏ maû.*
Peel (to),	*pŏ-p'i.*
Pencil, pen,	*pĭ.*
Pens and ink,	*pĭ-mĕ.*
People (the),	*pĕ-síng.*

Peppermint oil,	*pŏ-hó yiŭ.*
Perforate (to),	*c'hwēn-kwó c'hŭ.*
Perspire (to),	*c'hŭ-hán.*
Phœnix,	*fúng-hwáng.*
Pitcher,	*p'íng.*
Picture,	*hwá*
Pierce (to),	*chǎ.*
Pig,	*chū-tsż.*
Pigeon,	*pān-chiū.*
Pint measure,	*shīng.*
Pitfall,	*híen-k'ạng.*
Place (to),	*ngán-wán.*
Place,	*tí-fāng.*
Place of abode (polite),	*fù-sháng.*
Place stones,	*mán-shĭ-t'eŭ.*
Place beams,	*sháng-líang.*
Plain,	*c'hīng-pă.*
Plain stuffs,	*wŭ-hwā pú.*
Plain coloured cottons,	*wŭ-hwā sĕ-pú.*
Plaister,	*kau-yŏ.*
Plait (to),	*tà-pīen.*
Plane (to),	*p'aŭ.*
Planks of hard wood,	*chúng-mŭ pàn* (heavy).
Planks of soft wood,	*c'hīng-mŭ pàn* (light).
Please sit down,	*t'sìng-tsó.*

Plough (to),	*chīng, kặng·tiên.*
Poison,	*tŭ-yŏ.*
Politeness,	*lì-maú.*
Pongees,	*c'heû.*
Poor,	*tsién-c'hŭng (kiung).*
Port, jetty,	*kiāng-keù, mà-t'eû.*
Posterity,	*tsɀ̀-sặn.*
Posthumous title,	*sɀ̂-fă.*
Pour out tea,	*taù-c'hâ.*
Pour out wine,	*chèn-tsiù.*
Power,	*nặng-kán.*
Present (to),	*súng.*
Presents,	*lì-wŭ.*
Present tribute,	*tsín-kúng.*
Pretty,	*yiù-t'sū.*
Price,	*kiá-t'síen.*
Piece (a),	*p'ĭ.*
Pu, 240 sq. yards,	*meù.*
Pray for rain,	*k'iû-ù.*
Pray (to),	*taù-kaú.*
Prepare (to),	*ìŭ-peí*
Print (to),	*yín.*
Printed cottons,	*yīn-hwā pú.*
Prison,	*kícn-laû.*
Proceed forward (to),	*sháng-t'síen tseù.*

Proclamation,	*kaú-shí.*
Produce (to),	*shāng-cʻhŭ.*
Produce evidence (to),	*yìn-chíng.*
Profit,	*lí-sĭ.*
Promise (to),	*hŭ̀.*
Prosper (to),	*hīng-wáng.*
Pour out wine,	*chĕu-tsiù.*
Produce silk,	*tʻù-sź̄.*
Protect (to),	*paù-yiú.*
Proud,	*chīau-ngaú.*
Public duties,	*kŭng-shí.*
Pumpkin,	*tūng-kwā.*
Pump water,	*cʻhĕ-shuì.*
Purify, wash (to),	*sì.*
Purple,	*tʻīen-tʻsīng.*
Purposely,	*tʻĕ̆-i*
Pursue (to),	*chuī-kàn.*
Push (to),	*tʻuì.*
Push away,	*cʻhĕ̆.*
Put (to),	*kŏ̆.*
Put in tobacco.	*chwāng-yēn*
Put on mortar,	*tsí-sháng ni.*
Put on tiles,	*leì-pʻī.*
Putchuck,	*mŭ-hīang.*

Q.

Quail,	*ngān-c'hūn.*
Quarter of an hour,	*k'ĕ̆.*
Quickly, quick,	*k'waí-k'waí.*
Quicksilver,	*shuĭ-yín.*

R.

Racoon skín,	*laú-hwān p'í.*
Radishes,	*hûng-lô peĭ.*
Rail at persons (to),	*má-jín.*
Rain-water,	*yŭ̀-shuĭ.*
Raise water,	*tiaú-shuĭ.*
Rank and file,	*tuí-wŭ.*
Rare,	*nân tŏ.*
Rattans,	*shă̆-t'êng.*
Rattans stripped of bark,	*t'êng-jâng tsĭ̀.*
Raven,	*pă-ko.*
Raw,	*shặng.*
Raw buffalo hides,	*shặng-niú p'í.*
Raw cotton,	*míen-hwā.*
Read much,	*tī-k'án.*
Read (to study),	*tŭ.*
Ready, made ready,	*híen-c'hặng t'ī.*

Reap (to),	*sheŭ.*
Rebel (to),	*tsaú-fàn.*
Receive (to),	*sheú-shŏ.*
Receive blood,	*tsiĕ-hiŭ.*
Receive kindness,	*c'hêng-hwei.*
Receive customs,	*sheŭ-shui.*
Red,	*hûng.*
Red wood,	*hûng-mŭ.*
Redeem from sin,	*shŭ-tsui.*
Redeem (to),	*shŭ.*
Red-necked,	*hûng-pŏ qr.*
Redress grievances (to),	*shīn-yuēn.*
Reduce (to),	*chièn-c'hīng.*
Reeds,	*wei-tsz̀.*
Refine (to),	*lien.*
Reform (to),	*kai-chíng.*
Refuse,	*t'uī-t'sẑ.*
Refuse silk,	*twán-sz̄ t'eŭ.*
Refuse baroos camphor,	*sháng pīng-p'ién.*
Release (to),	*k'aī-shĭ.*
Rely on (to),	*k'aú.*
Remove (to),	*wô-túng.*
Remove (to),	*pān-chīa (kiă).*
Repair (to),	*siŭ.*
Repay (to),	*p'ei-hwân.*

Repent (to),	*hwei-kai.*
Reply (to),	*hwei-tă.*
Reply to letter (a),	*hwei-sin.*
Represent (to),	*tàng-tsó.*
Reprove (to),	*tsĕ-pei (pi).*
Reputation,	*ming-shīng.*
Rest (to),	*ngăn-sĭ, hiĕ.*
Retain (to),	*sheū-liŭ.*
Return (to),	*hwei-c'hĭ.*
Return money,	*hwân.*
Reverential,	*c'hiĕn-c'hêng.*
Reward,	*shàng.*
Rhinoceros,	*sz̄-niŭ.*
Rhinoceros skin,	*sz̄-p'î.*
Rhinoceros horns,	*sz̄-chiaù (kiŏ).*
Rhubarb,	*tá-hwâng.*
Rice,	*fán-mì.*
Ride horses (to),	*c'hí-mà.*
Ringed raven,	*laù-kwā.*
Ripe,	*shŭ.*
Rise, Raise (to),	*k'ì, (c'hi) (c'hì).*
Rise higher,	*chàng-c'hì lai.*
Rise in life,	*fă-tá.*
Roads,	*hán-lú.*
Rob and plunder,	*t'siang-tŏ.*

Rock crystal,	*shuì-tsīng.*
Root,	*pàn.*
Rose mallows,	*haī-teù k'eú.*
Rough persimmon,	*maū-shí.*
Row (to),	*tsíang, yaû.*
Royal title,	*wáng.*
Rub (to),	*mô.*
Rug,	*jŭ.*
Run (to),	*p'aû.*
Runner (a),	*kiŏ-fū.*

S.

Sable,	*tīau.*
Sacrifice,	*tsí.*
Sail,	*p'ung.*
Salt fish,	*híen-yû.*
Salted fowl eggs,	*híen-chī tán.*
Salted turnips,	*tá-t'eû t'saí.*
Salt-boat,	*yén-c'hwên.*
Salt water,	*híen-shuì*
Saltpetre,	*siaū.*
Salute,	*tsīng·ngāu.*
Same village,	*t'ûng-hīang.*
Samshoo (wine, spirit),	*chiù (tsiù).*

Sandal wood,	*t'ǎn-hīang.*
Sandal-wood ware,	*t'ǎn-hīang c'hí (k'i).*
Sand-fly,	*paĭ-líu.*
Sapan wood,	*sū-mŭ.*
Satin,	*twán-tsż.*
Satisfied,	*paù-liaù.*
Save,	*kiú.*
Saw, (a)	*chŭ.*
Say (to), speaking,	*shwŏ.*
Scallions,	*chiù-t'sai.*
Scatter,	*sán-k'aī.*
Scissors,	*tsżen-taū.*
Scoop,	*wǎ.*
Scull (to), (to row),	*yaû.*
Scull (a),	*lù.*
Sea-otter skin,	*haì-lûng p'í.*
Sea-horse teeth,	*haì-mà yâ.*
Seal character,	*chwén-wǎn.*
Seam, to sew,	*fûng.*
Seaweed,	*haì-t'sai.*
Secretary,	*shū-yŭ.*
Secretly inform,	*c'hwēn-t'ūng.*
See,	*k'án-chíen (kién).*
See (to),	*k'an, chaù-siûn.*
Seek (to),	*c'hǎ,*

Seize,	*nâ-chŏ.*
Seldom,	*nân-tĕ.*
Self,	*tsź-kĭ.*
Sell (to),	*maí.*
Send (to),	*tà-fă.*
Send habitually,	*c'haī-kwān.*
Send (a person),	*c'haī.*
Send (letter or parcel),	*kí.*
Sentence,	*kíّ, yĭ-kíّ-hwá.*
Separate (to),	*kĕ.*
Separate (to scatter),	*sán.*
Servant,	*yúng-jin.*
Serve (to),	*shí-féng, fŭ-sź.*
Service,	*kúng-yĭ.*
Sesamum oil,	*chĭ-mâ yiّ.*
Sesamum seed,	*chĭ-mâ.*
Set a cart in motion,	*k'aī-c'hē.*
Set out,	*pai-shĕ.*
Set on fire,	*fáng-hò.*
Seven,	*t'sĭ.*
Several tens,	*kĭ-shĭ.*
Shaft-mule,	*chiá-yuên ló-tsź.*
Shake (to),	*yaû.*
Shallow,	*t'sīen.*
Shanghae sycee, (98)	*kiù-pă yín.*

Shark,	*shā-û̂.*
Shark skins,	*shā-yû̂ p'i.*
Sharp, quick,	*k'waí.*
Shave (to), head,	*t'i, t'i-t'eû̂.*
Sheep,	*yâng.*
Sheep (appositive for),	*chĕ.*
Shelter thieves,	*wō-lîu.*
Shilling,	*sź-k'aī.*
Ship,	*c'hwên.*
Shirt,	*hān-shān.*
Shirtings (grey),	*pạn-sĕ yâng-pú.*
Shirtings (white),	*p'iaū-pĕ yâng-pú.*
Shoes,	*hiaî-tsź.*
Shop,	*tién-p'ú.*
Shore-plank,	*t'iaú-pàn.*
Short coat,	*twàn-shān.*
Shortness or length,	*c'hâng-twàn.*
Shut (to),	*kwān.*
Sick (to be),	*shạng-píng.*
Side of well,	*tsìng-pīen.*
Sign of possessive case,	*tĭ.*
Sign of the past,	*liaù.*
Silk, or woevn,	*sź̄, c'heū.*
Silk caps,	*c'heū-maú.*
Silk clothing,	*c'hεū ī-fŭ.*

Silk-worm,	*t'sán.*
Silk ribbons,	*sz̄-tai.*
Silk thread,	*sz̄-sien.*
Silure (a fish, sturgeon),	*nien-û.*
Silver,	*yin-tsz̀.*
Silver-mine ore,	*yín-k'wàng.*
Silver thread (real),	*chīn yín-sien*
Silver thread (imitated),	*chià yín-sien.*
Silver ware,	*yín-c'hi (k'i).*
Sing (to),	*c'húng.*
Singe (to),	*shaú-yên sai.*
Singing-lark,	*paí-ling.*
Sir,	*sīen-shēng.*
Sit in judgment,	*tsó-t'áng.*
Sit down,	*tsó-hia.*
Sit on the shaft (to),	*k'wá-yuên.*
Six,	*lǔ.*
Skin-rugs,	*pí-t'án.*
Skin and flesh,	*p'i-jǔ.*
Slap on the face,	*tà-tsui pá-tsz̀.*
Slip of paper,	*t'iau-chi.*
Slow, slowly,	*mán.*
Small bowl,	*û.*
Small city (district city),	*híen.*
Small fox-skins,	*siaù hû-lí-p'i.*

Smear,	*t'ŭ.*
Smile,	*hân-siaú.*
Smuggle,	*t'eū-shuí.*
Snuff,	*pĭ-yēn.*
Snuff candle,	*chiă-c'hü lă-hwā.*
Soda,	*kĩen.*
Soda vapour,	*kĩen-c'hí.*
Soft,	*míen-jwàn.*
Sole (a fish),	*pĭ-mŭ ŭ̂.*
Sometimes,	*yiù-shí.*
Son of heaven,	*t'ĩen-ts̀z.*
Soothe,	*ngăn-weí.*
Soul,	*sĩn-shín.*
South,	*nân.*
Sow discord,	*t'iaù-sō̆.*
Sow (to),	*chúng-tí.*
Sow thistle,	*k'ù-t'saí.*
Soy,	*tsíang-yiû̂.*
Speak (to),	*shwŏ-hwá.*
Spend (to),	*feí-yúng.*
Spelter,	*paĭ-c'hĩen.*
Spin (to),	*fàng-síen.*
Spinach,	*p'ŭ̂-t'saí.*
Spirit (wine)—ghost,	*tsiù,—kwei.*
Split rattans,	*t'ặng-jeú.*

L

Spoon,	*t'iaŭ-kǎng.*
Spotted stuffs,	*kweī-hwā pú.*
Spread dinner,	*paǐ-fún*
Spread mats,	*p'ū-sǐ.*
Spring,	*c'hūn.*
Spring-arrow,	*ti-nù.*
Sprinkle,	*shà c'hú.*
Square inch,	*fāng-tsún*
Square bricks,	*fāng-chwĕn.*
Square letters,	*fāng-tsź.*
Square table,	*fāng-chǒ.*
Square court,	*t'īen-tsìng.*
Squirrel-skin,	*hweī-shù p'i.*
Stairs,	*t'ī.*
Stand (to),	*chán.*
Start, 起	*c'hi-shīn.*
Start,	*k'aī c'hwên.*
Star aniseed,	*pă-chiaù.*
Statement,	*tān-tsź.*
Stay the night,	*t'sź-yé.*
Steel,	*kāng.*
Stick (to),	*t'iĕ.*
Sticklac,	*tsź-k'ēng.*
Starve (to die of hunger),	*ngó-sź.*
Steal,	*t'eú-t'sǐ.*

Step carefully,	*tseù-haù.*
Sting,	*t'sź.*
Stockings,	*wă-tsź.*
Stone,	*shĭ-t'eû.*
Stone-mason,	*shĭ-tsŏ.*
Stool,	*wŭ-tsź.*
Stop (to),	*t'ing.*
Storax,	*sū-hŏ yiû.*
Stove (a),	*hwò-lû.*
Style,	*wận-mĕ.*
Straight,	*yĭ-chĭ.*
Strange,	*shĕng.*
Straw shoes,	*t'saù-hiaî.*
Straw-hat braid,	*t'saù-maú pĭen.*
Straw brush,	*t'iaû-tsź.*
Streamer,	*fūng-sín c'hî.*
Strength,	*c'hí-lĭ.*
Stretch out the arm,	*shīn-pí.*
Strike,	*tà.*
Striped,	*sū-wận.*
Strong,	*laû.*
Study (to),	*t'ŭ-shū.*
Stupid,	*pận.*
Stupid,	*ngaí-pận.*
Suffering,	*nán.*

Sufficient,	*keú, tsŭ.*
Sugar-candy,	*pīng t'ǎng.*
Sulphur,	*liŭ-huáng.*
Summer,	*hía-t'iĕn.*
Sun (the),	*t'ai-yâng, jĭ-t'eú.*
Superabundance.	*yeù-ŭ.*
Superiors,	*chàng-peí.*
Surrender (to),	*t'eû-híang.*
Sustain (to),	*tàng.*
Swallow (a),	*yén-tsż.*
Swan,	*t'īen-ngô.*
Swear,	*fǎ-shí.*
Sweep,	*saŭ.*
Sword,	*taŭ.*

T.

Table,	*chŏ.*
Tael, two,	*lìang.*
Tailor,	*t'saí-fûng.*
Take away,	*nâ-k'ŭ.*
Take (to),	*nâ, pá.*
Take a letter,	*nâ-sín.*
Take care of,	*chaú-yíng.*
Take care of a house,	*k'ān fâng-tsż.*

Take dinner,	*c'hĭ-fán.*
Take up water,	*tà-shuì.*
Take in the mouth,	*híen.*
Take advantage of,	*c'híng.*
Tanned buffalo hides,	*sheû-niû-p'í.*
Tassels,	*weì-síen.*
Taste (to),	*c'hâng.*
Tauist temples,	*miaú-yǜ.*
Tea,	*c'hâ-yĕ.*
Teacup,	*c'hâ-wàn.*
Teach,	*kiaú-shū.*
Teach (to),	*chiaú (kiaú).*
Teacher,	*sīen-sāng.*
Tea warehouseman,	*c'hâ-chán.*
Teak planks,	*mâ-lĭ shú-pàn.*
Teapot,	*c'hâ-hû.*
Tear (to,)	*sz̄-p'ó.*
Telescope,	*t'sīen-lì chíng (kíng).*
Tempt,	*yiù-yeù, yiù-hwŏ.*
Ten,	*shì.*
Tenth of a dollar,	*kiŏ.*
Ten pints,	*teù.*
Ten strings,	*shĭ-tíau.*
Tent,	*cháng-făng.*
Thank (to),	*sié-sié.*

That,	*ná.*
That sort,	*ná-yáng.*
They,	*t'a-măn.*
There,	*ná-lĭ.*
There is,	*yiù.*
There, (Peking D.)	*ná-ăr.*
Therefore, or because,	*yīn-t'sż.*
These few,	*ché-sīe.*
Thick,	*heú.*
Thick robe,	*p'aû-tsż.*
Thimble,	*tì-chĕn.*
Thin,	*paŭ (pŏ).*
Thing,	*tŭng-sī.*
Think (to),	*siàng, sż-siàng.*
Thirst (to),	*k'ŏ.*
This,	*ché-kó.*
This year,	*kīn-nien.*
This sort,	*ché-yáng.*
Thou,	*nĭ.*
Three,	*sān.*
Three pure ones,	*sān-t'sīng.* (Tauist)
Three precious ones,	*sān-paù.* (Buddhist)
Three stories,	*sān-t'săng.*
Throw (to),	*sēng.*
Thrown silk,	*sz-chīng.*

Thus,	*ché-mò yáng.*
Tiger,	*laù-hù.*
Tiger's bones,	*hù-kŭ.*
Tiger-skins,	*hù-p'í.*
Tigers and panthers,	*hù-paú.*
Tight,	*chìn.*
Time, age,	*níen-kì.*
Tin,	*sĭ.*
Tinder,	*hò-jûng.*
Tin-plates,	*mà-k'eù t'iĕ.*
Tide,	*c'haû-shuì.*
Tired,	*sīn-k'ù.*
To,	*taú.*
Toad,	*há-mā.*
Toast (to),	*k'áng.*
Tobacco in leaf,	*yĕn-yĕ.*
To-day, (Peking D.)	*chīn-ạr, kĭn-t'iĕn.*
Together with,	*líen, t'ûng.*
To-morrow,	*míng-t'īen.*
Too,	*t'aí.*
Top of house,	*ŭ-tìng.*
Tortoiseshell,	*tai-mai.*
Tortoiseshell ware,	*lai-mí c'hí.*
Touch (to),	*mŏ.*
Towards, to,	*hiang, tüí.*

Trade,	shǎng-í.
Translate (to),	fān-í, fān⁻yǐ.
Travel with letters,	tseù-sín.
Treat (to),	k'án-tai.
Trees,	shú-mǔ.
Tremble (to),	fǎ-teù.
Trousers,	k'ǔ-tsz̀.
True,	chīn.
Truly,	shǐ-tsai.
Try (to),	shí-shí k'án.
Trowel,	ní-taū.
Twilled stuffs,	siě-u ǎn ṇ́ṷ.
Two English hours, (time)	shí-heú.
Two cups,	liang-peī.
Turkey,	hó-chī (kī).
Turmeric,	chīang-hwǎng.
Turnips,	lô-peǐ.
Turn back (to,)	hweí-chwèn.
Two,	ǎr, liang-kó.

U.

Umbrella,	ù-sán.
Unbleached,	pǎn-sě.
Under,	tì-hiá.

Under foot,	*chiŏ tì-hiú.*
Understand,	*tùng-tĕ.*
Unexpectedly,	*hwŭ-jên.*
Unmanufactured copper,	*shặng-t'úng.*
Unmanufactured iron,	*shặng-t'iĕ.*
Upon,	*sháng.*
Upper story,	*leû.*
Upright,	*twān-fāng.*
Upstairs,	*leû-sháng.*
Use (to),	*yúng.*
Use again,	*tsaí-t'ī.*

V.

Valuable,	*paù.*
Variegated kingfisher,	*feī-t'suí.*
Vegetable tallow,	*c'hiú-yiû.*
Vegetables and rice,	*t'saí-fán.*
Vegetable garden,	*i'saí-yuên.*
Velvet,	*hwā-tsìen jûng.*
Vermicelli,	*fèn-sƶ̄.*
Very,	*tsuí.*
Very many,	*haù-tō.*
Village (a),	*t'sặn, lī.*
Vinegar,	*t'sú.*

Violent,	*hiŭng.*
Virtuous (to be),	*wei-shén.*
Visiting card,	*p'ien-chì.*

W.

Wadded trousers,	*mien k'ú-tsż.*
Waistband,	*yaŭ-tai.*
Waistcoat,	*pei-sīn*
Wait,	*t'ing, tạng heú.*
Waiting-boy,	*siaù-sż.*
Wake,	*sìng, chiaú-sìng.*
Walk (to),	*tseù, tseù-lú.*
Walk far,	*tseù-yuèn.*
Walk for pleasure,	*yiú-wán.*
Wall,	*t'siång.*
Wall and moat,	*c'híng-c'hi.*
Want (to),	*yaú.*
War junk,	*chēn c'hwén.*
Warm,	*nwán.*
Warn,	*chìng-chié.*
Was,	*shí.*
Wash one's face (to),	*sż-lién.*
Waste,	*láng-fei.*
Waste time,	*t'eŭ-hien.*

Wasteful in expenditure, *feí-tsûn.*

Watches (èmaillés à
   perles),   *chū p̄ien shí-c'hín-p̀iau.*

Watch the house,   *k'án-chiā (kiā).*

Water   *shuì.*

Water (to),   *kīau-kwán.*

Water-melon,   *sī-kwā.*

Watch-ducks,   *k'ān-yă.*

Watches,   *shí-c'hín-p̀iau.*

Watchword,   *k'eù-haú.*

We,   *wò-mặn.*

Weather,   *t'īen-k'í (ch'í).*

Weave,   *chĭ-pú.*

Weep,   *k'ŭ.*

Weevil,   *wù-kŭ c'hûng,*

Weigh,   *c'híng.*

Weight,   *fặn-l̀iang.*

Well, good,   *haù.*

Well-water,   *ts̀ing-shuì.*

West of the capital, *chīng-sī (kīng).*

West of the lake,   *hû-sī.*

Westward,   *sī-p̄ien.*

Wet,   *shĕ.*

What,   *shén-mò;* pron. *shímmó.*

Wheat,   *s̀iau-mĕ.*

When,	*lì-shí.*
Where,	*nà-lí.*
Where ?	*nà-lì ?*
Which road ?	*nà-yǐ t'iaú-taú* (or *lú*).
White,	*pě.*
White eel,	*paǐ-shán.*
White-eyed thrush,	*hwá-meí.*
White elephant,	*pě-siang.*
White spotted shirtings,	*pě-tièn pú.*
White pepper,	*pě hû-tsiaŭ.*
White bicho de mar,	*pě haì-shén.*
White sharks' fins,	*pě yû-c'hí.*
White shirtings,	*pě-saǐ pú.*
White brocades,	*pè-t'í pú.*
White sugar,	*pè-t'âng.*
Whip,	*mà-pien tsǐ.*
Whole,	*t'suên.*
Whole life,	*chūng-shīn.*
Whole elephants' teeth,	*chèng siang-yâ.*
Wide,	*k'wān.*
Wife and children,	*kīa-kiuěn.*
Wild animals,	*yè-sheú.*
Wild elephant,	*yè-siang.*
Wild raw silk,	*yé-t'sân sǐ.*
Wild goose,	*tá-yén.*

Willing,	*k'ạng.*
Wind,	*fŭng.*
Window,	*c'hwāng-mặn.*
Wind and water,	*fŭng-shuì.*
Wine,	*tsiù.*
Window glass,	*pŏ-lí p'íen.*
Winter,	*tŭng-t'íēn.*
Winter (coarse) greens,	*pŏ-t'saí.*
With,	*hô, hwan, tûng, yúng.*
Withered,	*kān-k'ū.*
Within,	*lì.*
Wolf,	*lång.*
Women,	*fú-nừ.*
Won,	*yíng-liàu.*
Wonderful,	*hī-k'í.*
Wood (a piece of),	*mŭ-ạr, mŭ-t'eû.*
Wood for fuel,	*c'haí-sīn.*
Woollen yarn,	*jûng-síen.*
Woollen cloth,	*tá-ní.*
Worship (to),	*paí.*
Words,	*hwá, hwá-yü.*
Worth (to be),	*chĭ,*
Wound,	*shé-shāng.*
Woven silk,	*c'heû.*
Wrap,	*paū-chŏ.*

Wring dry,	*meù-kān.*
Write (to),	*siè.*
Written order,	*p'aí-p'iaú.*
Writer,	*taí-pĭ.*

Y.

Yam, the Chinese,	*shān-yò.*
Years,	*níen-kī.*
Years of age,	*suí.*
Yellow beeswax,	*hwâng-lă.*
Yellow bean sprouts,	*hwâng-teú yì.*
Yellow eel,	*hwâng-shán.*
Yellow lead,	*shĭ-hwâng.*
Yesterday,	*tsŏ-t'īen.*
You,	*ni-mặn.*
You may,	*k'ò-ì*
You must,	*tsùng-yaú.*
You must first,	*sīen-yaú.*
Young gentleman,	*kŭng-tsź.*
Your,	*líng.*
Your name,	*kweí-síng.*
Your home,	*kweí-tí.*
Your high name,	*kaū-síng.*

Your age,	*kwei-kăng.*
Your mother,	*ling-t'áng.*
Your son,	*ling-láng.*
Your wife,	*paū-kiūen.*
Your daughter,	*ling-ngai.*
Your business,	*kwei-kān.*
Your trade,	*kwei-yĕ.*

FINIS.